A DAY IN
PARADISE

A DAY IN PARADISE

LEIGH

McKNIGHT

This is a book of fiction. Characters, names and incidents are a product of the author's imagination.

Dedication

First, I thank God for all of his many blessings. I also thank my family and my friends for their love, understanding and support.

LEIGH McKNIGHT
Author of:
From My Front Porch
Sinners Never Sleep
Satisfying The Woman In Me/Satisfy
Satisfy 2
The Sun, The Sin and The Shame
A Day InParadise
A Day In Paradise 2
Emerging From His Shadow

Table of Contents

CHAPTER 1

That Thursday morning after having enjoyed a marathon of earth shattering, hanging naked from the ceiling lovemaking with Frank, the man of her dreams, Jordan Banks was reveling in the thought that what she'd just experienced was the closest thing to heaven that any girl could witness. And, yeah, Jordan felt fortunate to be that girl.

Four years ago while attending a friend's pool party, Jordan met Frank, a dark chocolate, motorcycle riding, hunk at that party. Sometime later, they fell in love and she loved him unconditionally ever since and to have that love reciprocated meant everything. Arriving at the party four years ago and seeing Jordan's heart stopping, jaw dropping curves clad in a lime green bathing suit lounging with friends poolside, he was certain he'd died and had gone straight to heaven because no one on earth was that perfect, he'd thought.

As he rolled off of her, she whispered between pants against his ear, "Promise me you'll never leave me."

"Where's that coming from?" He replied, without loosening his grip on her and struggling to catch his own breath.

"This feels so good—so right, I just don't ever want it to end," she cooed, running her hand over his rock hard chest.

"Baby, I ain't going nowhere," he assured her, completely exhausted and unwilling to do more than return to a blissful sleep, he closed his eyes and buried his head deeper into her neck.

"You promise?" She pressed.

"I promise." He drew her closer in his embrace and nestled in his powerful, muscular arms, within moments, she joined him in a very happy slumber.

Sometime later, dressed in lacy white panties, bra and matching robe that outlined her voluptuous curves, and her long, shapely legs stuck into tan strapped heels, Jordan returned to her bedroom carrying a steaming cup of coffee. She paused just inside the bedroom door and smiling contentedly, she watched Frank as he slept. The pale yellow sheet contrasting against his dark skin was down around his waist, exposing his broad chest while outlining his muscled legs and thighs under the sheet. She loved to feel the strength of his body pressed against hers, his legs wrapped around her, slamming himself into her, commanding and demanding things of her body that only he could and never had she disappointed. She loved everything there was to love about Frank. Everything!

Jordan walked over, placed the cup of coffee on the night table and sat on the side of the bed. She leaned in and whispered against Frank's ear, "Time to get up, sleepy head."

He turned over in bed to face Jordan, using the back of his hand to wipe sleep from his eyes. He stared at her. "Damn woman, you look good. Good enough to eat," he said appreciatively, reaching for her.

"Stop it," she said, gleefully, pushing his hands away and rising up from the bed. "If you don't get your behind out of that bed, we're gonna be late for work."

Frank snatched her hand, pulled her roughly which caused her to land on top of him in bed.

"Frank," she began but her protests were interrupted by his mouth in a kiss that was fierce, passionate. He licked her lips, nibbled them, sucked them before devouring them with his mouth. Then, his tongue was inside her mouth, probing, seeking finding exactly what he was searching for. Their tongues began that aged old dance. It wasn't long before she was drawn in again, deeply and sinking deeper with every passing second, relishing the passion-filled kiss she'd gotten used to from him and enjoying it far too much for anything else to matter. Frank had that power over her. He had the ability to make her want him excessively. Need him desperately. Love him tirelessly, and she never wanted it to end.

Frank quickly pushed Jordan's robe away from her shoulders and down her body as he unhooked her bra. As the fabric fell away, exposing the naked flesh of her firm breasts, it was difficult to draw his eyes away before he began to plant a trail of wet kisses. He cupped her breasts with his hands and used his thumbs to run over the soft pebbles, feeling them harden under his touch. When his mouth came down hard to claim one luscious nugget and began a fever pace of nibbling, licking, sucking, it took her breath away. She closed her eyes helplessly as her ears rang by the beating of her own blood coursing through her veins. His mouth went from one breast to the next, taking in shocking mouthfuls of her firm flesh. The sensation of his mouth devouring her breasts set off fires of desire deep inside her. She closed her eyes as she abandoned herself to the heated assault of his mouth on her.

His hands moved down her soft, sleek body, pushing down the lace fabric that clung to her round, voluptuous hips. "Damn." He gazed down at her, "I love this body. I love looking at it, feeling it, the way you give it to me. Woman, you drive me crazy," he said, hoarsely, his eyes dazed with unmistakable passion.

Completely naked underneath him, he ran his hands feverishly over her body. He kissed her again, probing his tongue deep inside her mouth and as her tongue greeted his, the most animalistic duel began. His mouth moved to her breasts, then the indention of her navel where he used the tip of his tongue to tease her there. As his mouth travelled to the prize, the hairless mound between her thighs that always managed to drive him completely insane, she trembled and whimper with an insatiable need, an undeniable desire for this man to have her, take all of her.

He sucked greedily on the soft bulb while his fingers parted her feminine folds. His tongue slid deep into her soft center that was already wet and throbbing and urging him to take what he wanted, what she wanted him to have, to take everything. Her legs automatically went over his shoulders and she moved her body against his hot, demanding mouth, igniting his passion in a more demanding way. There, he sucked on her fiercely, unyieldingly, enjoying her juices that flowed freely.

Frank moved back up Jordan's body, his heart racing out of control. When their bodies were perfectly aligned, he wrapped his hands in her hair pulling her closer to him and with the force of a runaway train, he shoved his hardened, enormous penis into her pulsating cavity, filling her core while a long, continuous moan escaped her.

"Give it to me, baby. Give it all to me," he sang, huskily against her ear.

As Frank slammed into Jordan grinding hard and furiously into her, she met his forceful thrusts with her own forceful moves. As they moved against each other, her body gripped him, held him, causing him to chew down on his bottom lip, so hard that he drew blood. As he continued to plunge savagely into her, she withered and bounced as her moans went from animal-like whimpers to outright screams.

Frank buried his mouth in the creamy flesh between her breasts. "I love you, baby. I will always love you," he whispered as he kissed and nibbled her. When she lifted her legs and wrapped them tightly around his waist, his pace accelerated and he plunged into her with a colossal ferociousness that sent waves of shocking pleasure careening through her thrashing, perspiration drenched body.

Overwhelmed with the shudders of pleasure rushing through him, he gathered her tightly in his arms and rode her into complete and absolute satisfaction before releasing everything into her that was left inside him before rolling off of her.

Immediately afterward, Jordan and Frank leaped out of bed and giggling like love struck teenagers, they raced to the bathroom, showered, got dressed and raced out of the house. They kissed once more through the opened window of her late model silver Altima. She pulled on an ear lobe, driving off watching Frank from her rear view mirror as he curled his legs around his motorcycle and gunned it down the street. Jordan hated that motorcycle and didn't bother to hide her disappointment the day he showed it off. Actually, she didn't hate the motorcycles as much as she hated the wild and crazy things Frank did when he rode his motorcycle. He rode it too hard, too fast and he took too many risks.

Arriving at Cherokee High School where the twenty-nine year old taught Math, Jordan pulled into a designated teacher's parking space. She grabbed her purse and laptop from the passenger seat and hurried into the office, where she signed in and had just closed her classroom door when the final school bell rang.

"Good morning, class," Jordan called out throwing her purse in a drawer and laying her laptop on her desk. She glanced across the classroom and noticed Moses Dingle and his best friend, Tyler Murray, two students who were always getting into some situation, snickering while Moses was trying to conceal a magazine under his shirt that they'd been looking in before Jordan arrived.

"Which one of you would like to put the first problem from your homework assignment on the blackboard this morning?" Jordan asked. When none of the students replied, she said, "Don't all of you volunteer at the same time." Then, walking between two rows of seats, she stopped in front of Moses. "What about you?" She inquired.

"Ms. Banks, we only have one day left of school this year, why do we still have to do homework assignments when everybody else around here is chillin'?"

Some of the students snickered.

Ignoring the comment, Jordan said, "Oh yeah, I think Moses wants to put the first problem on the board and share with us how he arrived at his answer. But before you do that, Moses why don't you let me hold onto that magazine you have hidden inside your shirt until the end of class."

The students snickered again. Moses made a face as he removed the magazine and handed it to Jordan before getting out of his seat with his homework assignment in hand, walked up to the board and wrote the math problem on it.

When he was finished, Jordan asked the class, "Do you all see how Moses arrived at that answer?"

"Yes, Ms. Banks," the students replied in unison.

"Are there any questions?"

"No, Ms. Banks."

"Alright then. Good job, Moses. Now, who would like to go next?"

Jordan breezed through her morning classes and was on her way to lunch when her cell phone attached to her belt vibrated. She pulled it from the hook and checked the number. It was Sarah Benjamin, Frank's mother. When Jordan answered her phone,

Sarah had already hung up. Jordan returned the call. It went to Sarah's voice mail.

Jordan entered the cafeteria, picked up a tray and moved through the line where she ordered potatoes and gravy, fried chicken, corn, an apple and a glass of sweet tea. Then, with the tray in her hands, she left the cafeteria, entered the teachers' lounge and joined her friends at a table.

"Hello, Ladies," Jordan greeted Samantha and Maggie happily, putting her tray down on the table before taking a seat next to Samantha.

"Hello, Diva," Samantha replied, forking a piece of tomato from her chef salad into her mouth while eyeing the fitted navy blue dress Jordan was wearing. "I see you made the dress. It is hot."

"It sure is," Maggie agreed, taking a sip from her tea glass.

"Thanks. I made it a couple of days ago," Jordan answered.

"You are wearing it too, girlfriend. It looks great on that body of yours," Samantha complimented, forking more salad into her mouth."

"I don't know how you do it," Maggie said. "It takes special skills to see an outfit, cut it out and make the garment without a pattern."

Samantha changed the subject, crowing excitedly, "I can't wait until tomorrow when school will be over and in a couple of days, get my ass on that cruise ship. Um, um, um."

"Ocho Rios, here we come, baby," Maggie said and bit into her hamburger.

"I'm going to forget about everyone, all the things that need to be done around my house, and I'm going to chill out and enjoy myself. This has been one heck of a year and this trip is exactly what I need right now," Samantha said, and looked at Jordan. "Sure wish you were coming with us."

"Yeah, girl. Jamaica is going to be such fun," Maggie stated. "I told you I've got some extra cash. You could fly over and join us."

"And, I'll be happy to pitch in," Samantha offered, sipping her soft drink.

"That is so sweet, you two, and I really appreciate the offer," Jordan looked from one friend to the other, "but I'm not taking money from either of you. My budget is so tight, I couldn't afford to pay you guys back."

She grinned putting a fork of potatoes into her mouth.

It would be nice to have the freedom, the luxury to be able to do some fun, devil may care things every once in a while but eleven years ago after their mother died, Jordan became the caretaker of Stephanie and Steven, her twin siblings, providing them with everything they needed and could afford, although Steffie always wanted more. Much more. And, as she grew older, Steffie developed an amazing over the top shopping addiction, always charging more than they could afford, with Jordan just barely being able to pay the minimum monthly amount required. The one thing their mother had stressed was that they receive a good education. And, Jordan had seen to it.

The twins had now graduated college more than a year and in the next six months, Jordan would turn over to them, repayment of their student loans, then she could one day see having a little extra money in her own pockets.

"Now, if I were selling my own designs, I'd be on that cruise ship with you two. Heck, I'd probably own one. One on a smaller scale of course," she joked and they all chuckled.

"I wouldn't be mad at you," Samantha said, then directed a sly glance at Jordan. "I saw you rushing in here this morning just before the final bell. Another hot night with that tall, dark and fine as hell piece of dark man meat?"

"Heeeyyy." Maggie pumped her fists in the air.

Jordan chuckled and winked at her.

"He certainly is one good looking bald headed brotha," Samantha said.

"Uh huh," Maggie agreed.

"I have such a damn erotic fixation on him." Jordan rubbed her knees together under the table, excitement bubbled up inside her as she returned a sly glance of her own, remembering what took place between her and Frank in her bed the past twenty-four hours. "That man is a beast and I'm so in love with him." She blushed. "He was all over me all last night and back at it again this morning. He's so intense and I love that."

"Yeesss." Maggie pumped her fist again. "He looks like one of those all night long brothas, the kind of man who grabs your hair, buries your face in a pillow and just goes for it."

"Yeah, gurrrl."

"He just can't seem to get enough of that thing huh?" Maggie chuckled. "You must be walking around with kryptonite between those legs."

The three ladies chuckled.

"Sounds like he's tearing that thing up every chance he gets," Samantha giggled.

"Uh huh." Jordan giggled, lifting a piece of chicken to her mouth. "Actually, Frank could make a sex slave out of me. But guess what? I'd willingly accommodate him and love every second of it."

"I know that's right," Samantha chuckled.

"That's what I'm talking about." Maggie reached over and gave Jordan the high five.

"I can't help it that the man has his shit together not to mention he's so damn hot," Jordan said, just as her cell phone vibrated. She wiped her mouth with her paper napkin and unhooked the phone from her belt. "Hello," she answered.

"Jordan, I'm so glad I finally got you," the caller said, tearfully.

"Mrs. Benjamin." Jordan swallowed hard, hearing the anxiety in her voice and asked, "Is something wrong?"

"Have you heard from Frank today?" Mrs. Benjamin asked.

Jordan's smile begun to fade. "Not since this morning. Why? What's going on?" She wondered whether Frank had been involved in an accident on his motorcycle. Was he in a hospital? Or worst? She felt herself becoming frantic. She'd warned him countless times to be careful riding his bike, to not take so many chances but had he listened to her warnings? Absolutely not. It seemed the more she mentioned her concerns, the more he was determined to be more daring.

Now only moments away from full blown panic, Jordan whispered, "That damn motorcycle." Then she asked, "Is Frank alright, Mrs. Benjamin?"

Sarah Benjamin took in a deep breath, blew her nose and told Jordan the reason for her call. Her words cut into Jordan's heart like a knife rendering her speechless.

Jordan's mouth and eyes flew opened as shock stole through her mind, her body. Moments later, she felt her breath escape. It was then she realized that she'd been holding it.

She tried to erase the words racing around inside her head. Her stomach was in knots, her heart pounded and as she rose out of her seat, her legs began to quiver to the point where she feared they wouldn't hold her up as she walked away from her friends. One shaky hand clutched the phone to her ear while the other rested against her chest. She walked outside the room and leaning against the wall, she squeezed her eyes shut; bracing herself and hoping the words would be different this time when she asked, "What did you say?"

Mrs. Benjamin repeated her comment.

Tugging at her ear lobe, Jordan struggled to maintain some semblance of calm. She asked, "What are you talking about? Frank and I were together until he left my place this morning."

"I don't know how something like this could've happened." Sarah sniffed again. "I've been trying to reach him all morning but I'm getting his voice mail."

Jordan felt a chill run the course of her body as the impact of what she'd just heard settled around her shoulders. "Let me see if I can find out what's going on with him."

"Frank loves you, Jordan that's why none of this makes any sense," Sarah said, then asked, "Are you alright?"

"No, I'm not alright," Jordan said, feeling numb. "If what you say is true, I want to kill that bastard, yet on the other hand, I feel strangely relieved."

"Relieved?" Sarah was confused.

"I thought Frank had gotten hurt on that stupid motorcycle."

After a moment, Sarah Benjamin said, "for what it's worth, Jordan, I know exactly how you must be feeling."

Without a moment's hesitation, Jordan said as tears welled up in her eyes, "No you don't, Mrs. Benjamin. You have no idea."

Jordan ended that call and immediately placed a call to Frank. Voice mail. After a few seconds, she placed a second call, then a third but again, each call went to his voice mail. When she rejoined her friends, the devastated look on her face didn't go unnoticed.

Samantha stared at Jordan. "What's wrong?" She inquired, putting her fork on her plate and touching her mouth with her napkin. "Did something happen?"

"Jordan?" Maggie's face, covered with concern as she awaited the answer.

Jordan's head was spinning as she reclaimed her seat at the table. She felt she was going to be sick; everything was moving too fast yet moving in slow motion at the same time.

"You look like you were hit by a truck," Samantha said.

"What's going on?" Maggie asked, perched on the edge of her seat.

"Frank got married today." Jordan's lips quivered as she choked back a sob while her friends looked on in shocked surprise.

Jordan was rattled, emotionally wrecked, but she managed to get through the next couple of hours. At the end of the school day, she grabbed her purse and laptop and she stormed out to her car. The betrayal Frank brought into her life clung to her like a cheap, wet suit and all she wanted was rip it off, burn it and bring back some sanity into her life. She needed to get home. To be alone. Alone so she could think. Scream. Break things. Then scream some more.

She climbed into her car, threw her purse and laptop on the passenger seat and started the engine. She put the gear in Reverse and backing out the parking space, she saw one of her students running toward her and waving her hand.

"Miss Banks," the student called out.

Jordan stopped her car and put the gear in Park. She composed her features and forced herself to smile as she rolled down the window. "Asia, you need a ride home?"

"No, Miss Banks. My cousin is waiting for me," Asia said, jerking a thumb towards the car parked in the students' parking space. "I wanted to say goodbye in case I don't see you tomorrow, but I especially wanted to thank you for helping me with my Math this semester. I wouldn't be graduating this year without your help, Miss Banks."

"You are more than welcome, Asia, but you did the majority of the work."

Asia shook her head definitively. "Seriously, Miss Banks, you helped me a lot, so thank you and I hope you have a great summer."

Jordan knew she'd have anything but a great summer, but she smiled and said, "Thank you. You have a great summer as well."

"I still say that's the coolest watch ever," Asia complimented Jordan's watch as she'd done every time she saw it. "Bye, Miss Banks." She turned and was about to rush off.

Jordan looked at the watch on her wrist. Frank had given it to her for Christmas two years ago and she loved it. "Asia," she called out, removing the watch from her wrist. Asia turned and walked back to the car. "Here, take it. It's yours." She handed Asia the watch.

"Miss Banks," Asia said in surprise, "I can't take your watch."

"You're not taking it. I'm giving it to you. Consider it a graduation gift."

"Are you sure?"

"I'm sure."

Asia's eyes went bright with joy as she accepted the gift from her benefactor, and she slipped it on. "This is awesome." She examined how the watch looked on her wrist.
"Enjoy it."

"I will. Thank you." Asia reached through the car window and hugged Jordan. "Bye, Miss Banks." She then rushed off to the waiting car.

Jordan left the parking lot. On the way home, she tried several times to reach Frank but her calls continued to go to his voice mail. How could something like this happen? She wondered.

Frank owned a welding shop on the other side of town and though they saw each other almost every night, there were times when he came late and left early, received endless phone calls unless he turned off his phone, and Jordan noticed that he'd begun drinking more and he didn't initiate intimacy as often as he once did. She assumed that was because he spent an enormous amount of time at work, he was always exhausted, and she'd let it go at that.

Jordan tugged at her ear lobe as she pulled into her garage. She closed the garage door and after shutting off the engine to her car, an unrecognizable scream tore its way from her throat as she wailed while pounding the steering wheel. "How could you do this to me?" She choked out, tears flowing down her cheeks. Her body was racked by pain, indescribable pain, the kind of pain she'd never experienced before, the kind of pain that only time would heal.

Sometime later, Jordan pulled herself together, exited her car and entered her house through the kitchen door. She entered her bedroom, dropped her purse, laptop and keys on the dresser and removed her clothes, allowing them to fall to the floor. She took a long shower, returned to her bedroom, slipped into a pair pajamas and feeling completely drained; she climbed into bed with the intention of laying there about an hour. Turning onto her side, her eyes went to the picture on the night table beside her bed. Frank's picture. Fresh tears welled up in Jordan's eyes again and flowed down her cheeks. She stared at the picture a moment longer before she lifted it from the night table, turned it face down and put it back on the table. That was the last thing she remembered until sometime later when she was awakened by the sound of voices. *Frank*, she thought rising up in bed, expecting to see him. Instead, it was Steffie and Steven who entered her bedroom.

Steven's fingers were busy checking his internet device. "Wad up, Sis?" He said, going over to sit in a chair in the corner of the room.

"Hey you guys," Jordan said, rubbing her eyes.

"Why are you in bed so early," Steffie asked, going over to kiss Jordan on her cheek before plopping down on the bed. "Are you alright?"

"I'm good," Jordan replied with no intentions of sharing with her siblings what happened between her and Frank. She wasn't ready for questions she knew they'd have that she didn't have answers to.

Steven slipped his phone into his pants pocket, picked up the TV remote from the bed and turned the channel to ESPN to get a recap of the sporting events of the day before returning to his seat.

Keeping up her bubbly, happy-go-lucky spirit she was known for, Jordan asked, looking from one to the other, "What are you two doing here?"

"We used to live here, remember?" Steffie chuckled, giving her sister a comical look.

"We told you we were coming by," Steven said. "Or did you forget?"

Ignoring her brother's comment, Jordan said, "So tell me about Florida."

"Florida was great," Steffie answered, excitedly. "We partied our asses off."

"I just bet you did."

"It was non-stop. We had to come home just to get a little rest," Steffie chuckled.

"What about you, old man?" Jordan directed her question to her brother.

Toying with an object he picked up from the table near him, Steven said, "Ahhh sis, you couldn't stand it if I told you." He and Steffie chuckled.

After listening to her siblings' accounts of their time spent in Florida, Jordan blew out a puff of air, then said, "Well, I'm glad you two enjoyed your time away. What are your plans now? I'm not rushing you but I want to know that you two are making some definite plans about your future."

"We're working on some things," Steffie stated.

"Tell me about it," Jordan said with a concerned look engraved in her brow.

"Aaaaw, there she goes again," Steffie said as she and Steven gave each other a look. "Always worrying about one thing or another."

"Tell me what you're working on." Jordan looked from Steffie to Steven.

"We're buying a house," Steffie answered.

"Really?" Jordan was surprised. They hadn't mentioned buying a house before. Where? Are you two making enough to take on the expense of owning a house?"

"Good grief, there you go giving us the third degree again," Steven teased.

"We're good," Steffie said.

Jordan gave her brother a look. "When is this supposed to happen?"

"We'll have you over soon, after we get the place fix up a bit," Steffie answered.

Jordan relented. "Well, good luck. You guys are grown and have your own lives to live."

"You're not gonna try and stop us?" Steven asked.

"She is taking this better than I thought," Steffie said to her twin brother.

"I told you I thought she might be alright with it," Steven said.

"You did but I wasn't sure. You know Jordan. She still has those maternal instincts," Steffie said, then added, "I'll bet old Frank is gonna be happy that Steven and I aren't gonna try to move back in here."

Jordan felt fresh pain ripped through her chest at the thought of hearing Frank's name.

"Yeah, that lousy mother fucker," Steven muttered under his breath. He'd never liked Frank and always felt his sister could do so much better, but he always acted civil toward him because he knew how his sister felt about Frank. No accounting for taste, Steven always whispered when he saw his sister and Frank together.

Jordan wasn't going to talk about Frank. Instead she got out of bed asking, "Are you guys hungry?"

"I'm starved," Steven said, and they went off to the kitchen.

Jordan didn't hear from Frank that night and by morning, she was certain that what his mother told her about him the day before was true. What she wasn't able to wrap her mind around was how he could spend the night making love to her, then leave her bed the following morning and without a single word, marry someone else.

Jordan reported for the last day of work and was met by Samantha and Maggie before she could get out of her car.

"Jordan, how are you, girl?" Maggie asked as Jordan got out of her car. "I was worried when I couldn't reach you last night. Why didn't you call me?"

"I'm sorry. It just wasn't a good night."

"Have you heard from Frank?" Samantha inquired.

Jordan closed the car door. "No."

"So do you think he really married someone else?" Samantha asked.

"I'm certain he did," Jordan replied, sadly as they approached the building.

"What happened, Jordan? Why would he do something like that?" Samantha wanted to know.

"I have no idea. I thought things were great between us. I see now just how wrong I was. He really had me fooled but the real betrayal was him not telling me what his intentions were."

"And he hasn't even called with an explanation? That shows what a piece of shit he is," Maggie said. "Seriously, this demonstrates his character one hundred percent."

"It appears that I was no more than just a side piece to him." Jordan was incredulous.

"I'm clutching my pearls, darling," Samantha said, rolling her eyes.

"I can't believe this. You've been his ride or die chick, been faithful all these years to his black ass," the feisty Maggie said. "Who does that?"

They entered the building and walked down the hall.

"He needs his ass whipped by some big ass dude with big ass fists for pulling some shit like that," said Maggie, seething quietly so no one else would hear their conversation. "That son of a bitch."

"He's an idiot for not realizing what a gorgeous badass twenty-nine year old babe you are," Samantha said. "He's a damn fool." Then looking at her watch, she said, "I gotta go. You want to go somewhere for drinks later? Maggie and I want to spend some time with you before we go on the cruise day after tomorrow."

"Yeah," Maggie cosigned. "We can celebrate having this school year bchind us, have some good drinks and do some serious male bashing. Hell, I'm ready to get turnt. Let's go out, have a good time and forget his ass."

"I'm all about that," Samantha said. "It'll be lit."

"I appreciate it, girls but I don't think so. I'm not up to it," Jordan declined the offer.

"Ahh, come on," Samantha urged. "Why go home to an empty house when you can hang out with us and do some real damage. Maybe even pick up a cute brotha or two."

"I'm ready to turn up the fun," Maggie assured.

Jordan looked thoughtful for a moment. Then she lifted her shoulders and said, "Alright, but I don't want to be out too late. I'm exhausted."

"Gurrlll, let's do this. You can rest when you are dead." Maggie chuckled.

Jordan and Samantha joined in.

"Okay," Jordan said. "I'll see you ladies after work."

At 1:15 that afternoon, Jordan left her classroom and after final goodbyes to other co-workers, she exited the building and went outside to find Samantha and Maggie waiting by her car.

"Where are we going?" Samantha asked as the three of them climbed into Jordan's car and fastened their seatbelts.

"Let's go to Monty's," Maggie suggested.

"Great, I love Monty's," Samantha exclaimed eagerly.

A short time later, Jordan, Samantha and Maggie entered Monty's, a night club and restaurant.

They ordered club sandwiches, chips and sweet tea with Jordan eating only a small bite of her sandwich.

"You know, I try to be sensible about life. I don't try to make myself believe things that I know aren't true. While I thought Frank loved me, I never once thought I was the only woman he was seeing."

"What?" Maggie exploded.

"Maggie, get real!" Jordan said. "The ratio of women to men is like seven to one and with those odds, I'd really be a fool to think that I'm the only woman in my man's life. Women would like to believe that, but I believe the majority of men have flings; some of them are so slick with their crap that a lot of women don't know, some women do know but turn a blind eye. Yet, there are those who deal with cheating husband who treat them well and figure that they'd rather have that than a no good man who treats them like crap, but what Frank did…."

"Yeah, how's that working for you?" Maggie snapped.

Ignoring Maggie's comment, Samantha said, "I never had it in me to admit that to myself before, because I'd hate the thought of my man cheating on me."

"No one likes it, Sam," Jordan answered, "but that is just how it is sometimes."

After the meal, Samantha and Maggie talked about getting their hair and nails done for their trip and they talked about how Jordan would move on without Frank. Later, they went into the club where they danced, ordered shots and danced some more. Then, after having coffee, around eight o'clock, Jordan drove Samantha and Maggie back to school to pick up their cars.

CHAPTER 2

One week after the unforeseen betrayal and just as the sunrise announced the dawning of a brand new day; Jordan picked herself up from a hotel couch in Montego Bay, where

she'd spent the past six days. She
walked over to the bed, pulled from
the suitcase that had remained
unpacked since she arrived in Jamaica,
a one piece green bathing suit that
perfectly matched her emerald eyes
and slipped it on. She pulled her long,
bone straight, auburn hair up in a pony
tail, accentuating her oval shaped face
with high cheekbones, a small nose
and perfectly shaped lips over pearly
white teeth. She stuck her dainty feet
into a pair of flip flops and after
tossing a large beach towel, sketch
pads, pencils and a bottle of water into
her handbag, she left her hotel room
and headed towards the ocean.

Jordan walked along the beach
behind huge sunglasses that concealed
eyes that'd been red and swollen from
hours of crying. She couldn't make
herself believe that Frank had hurt her
so badly, that he didn't even have the
decency to inform her of his intentions

face to face or through a simple phone call. Jordan had never known pain of that magnitude existed. She slapped away tears that slid from her beautiful almond shaped eyes and ran down her cheeks.

On the beach, Jordan encountered a few people coming and going, they all appeared happy. Observing each person who passed by her, it became evident that it was up to her ensure her own happiness. Why would she continue to allow herself to suffer because of someone else's inability to love her as she did him and who could so easily walk away from her without the decency of letting her know? No. Jordan didn't deserve what happened to her but then, many people don't deserve what happened to them. That was life and who said life was fair. She'd just get over it, put on her big girl panties and keep it moving. That was what she'd thought but would it actually be that easy.

Jordan dropped her handbag on the white sandy beach, removed the towel and just as she was about to spread it on the ground, she cast her eyes out toward the turbulent blue-green waters when suddenly, her eyes popped open. She held the towel with one hand and used the other hand to push her sunglasses back on top of her head and she unashamedly watched the tall, handsome, stranger as he emerged out of the ocean. It was as though the waters parted for him to make his exit.

There wasn't a single cloud in the sky yet Jordan was certain she'd heard thunder clap inside her head while her entire body exploded from a huge bolt of lightning that escaped through her toes. She was spellbound as her eyes trailed over the stranger's body; his broad shoulders, sculpted arms and abs and biceps not only powerful enough to make Mr. Universe weep but no hot blooded woman who saw them would ever forget them.

Her attention lingered on the stranger's thighs that looked firm and muscled and his powerful, athletic legs that moved with such authority that it took her breath away. When she was able to breathe again, she exhaled so forcefully that the air flew from her lungs in a large puff causing her to suddenly feel light headed.

Wow, she thought, staring at the stranger. *Either that man is right out of some damn dream or I'm hallucinating.*

Reluctantly, Jordan tore her gaze away from him but only for an instant, just long enough to spread out her towel on the beach, sit and dump out the other items from her bag. Her eyes were drawn back to the gorgeous hunk as she reached blindly for her pad and pencils. As that wonderful ripple in the atmosphere walked in her direction with water dripping from his body, Jordan held boldly in her gaze the supersize order of bronze decadence. Despite her pain and exhaustion, Jordan felt exhilarated as excitement stirred in her stomach. Though she tried to downplay what was happening inside her, she was quick to note that not only was there something about the stranger that screamed sex appeal, perfection from the strong angle of his jaw right down to his toes that left deep imprints in the sand as he walked along the beach but there was something about him that touched everything deep inside her.

When he was only a few feet away, their eyes met. And WHAM. Their eyes locked and remained locked. He held her stare until her brain ordered her to look away, only the rest of her body disobeyed. There was an explosion that rushed the course of her body, a torrent of warmth seeped through her. She'd never been affected by anyone that way before. Not even Frank, and he had affected her in ways that she couldn't describe. Yet, this was different. Jordan found herself transfixed by his tall, well-built body and mesmerized by his liquid brown eyes.

As the stranger walked past Jordan, their eyes continued to hold each others, caressed each others. He had the most gorgeous eyes she'd ever seen only they were also the saddest eyes she'd ever seen and she wondered why he was so sad. What had happened in his life that'd cause him such sadness? Had someone deceived him as she'd been deceived?

Suddenly, she felt compelled to look away but not before she thought she saw his face soften ever so slightly and a hint of a smile touch the corners of his lips. Jordan shook her head to clear the illicit thoughts she was experiencing. No matter how powerful their connection appeared, there was no way she'd come to foreign soil and get involved with some handsome stranger, only to have him walk away from her as easily as Frank had. Absolutely not! But, looking at that magnificent creature couldn't hurt and she certainly appreciated the view.

This was Jordan's last day on the island and she was going to enjoy it even though there was a terrible inferno of Frank and now this stranger racing around inside her head. Collecting her thoughts, she pulled her sunglasses back down on her face and began to sketch.

Walking along the beach with the feel of cool sand under his feet, the stranger couldn't get the woman out of his mind who he'd just seen sitting on the beach. She was the most beautiful woman he'd ever seen only she looked so sad. He wondered w*hy someone so beautiful was so sad.* He turned and glanced over his shoulder to see her writing on a pad. After walking a little further away from her, he sat on the sand and turned to stare at her. She was breathtaking. He wondered whether she was alone, would someone be joining her; a husband, a lover nearby, a friend? Surely not a husband. No man in his right mind would be okay with his wife being out on the beach alone looking like that. *She was a goddess*, he thought, remembering the way that bathing suit clung to her gorgeous body and the legs attached to that body. Incredible!

He surely would like to get to know her better.

He uttered to himself, "I don't know who you are but one thing I know for sure is that I'm going to get to know you. I have to." *Only not right away*, he thought.

Two days after learning of Frank's betrayal and one day after school ended for the summer, Jordan had packed her bags and as her friends boarded the cruise ship for Ocho Rios, she charged a trip to an almost maxed out credit card and boarded a plane that took her from Augusta, Georgia to Montego Bay, Jamaica, on a vacation that she couldn't afford. Losing Frank had become too difficult to cope with so Jordan decided to distance herself from him and leave the pain far behind. But, after spending almost a week on this gorgeous, vibrant island, the pain in her heart was as strong as ever. Any other time, she would've enjoyed beautiful powder blue skies over floral-scented breezes floating across the ocean, caressing her skin and she would've smiled graciously at the appreciative and longing looks that were being lavished upon her by so many admirers that had now come out on the beach.

Jordan was deeply in love with Frank, the handsome six feet, bald headed, close-cut bearded man. He'd been an incredible lover who'd brought love to her heart and unbelievable passion to her bed. Even now, just thinking about him still brought a sharp shudder of desire that shook Jordan to her core. Yes! Frank had been her ideal man—the man she thought she'd marry, have his children and spend the rest of her life with.

Most of her life she'd been looking for love and with Frank, she thought she'd finally found it. At least that was what she'd thought, what she'd hoped. But, she'd picked the wrong man to love and he'd hurt her to her very soul.

Staring out across the ocean, a fresh crop of tears formed in her eyes as she was remembering how he'd wrapped her in his arms, held her tight and whispered sweet promises to her, promises she knew now that he had no intention of keeping.

She was certain this stranger was the kind of man who also got what he wanted and she felt certain it was without pretending to be something he was not, unlike Frank and the situation he created that she found herself running away from.

After drawing a few lines on her sketch pad and unable to concentrate, she put her pad and pencil down and looked out on the rippling blue waters.

"May I join you," a masculine voice asked.

She stiffened, snapping back to reality as she brushed aside a tear and looked up warily through her glasses at the brazen intruder who, without an invitation, had already plopped himself down on her towel.

She was taken aback by his boldness. She replied, "Excuse me."

"I saw you from the hotel window and I had to get a closer look to see if you really were as gorgeous as you appeared from there," he began, and she rolled her eyes behind her sunglasses. She had heard it before, all of the variations from guys, coming at her, some trying to get a quick hit it and quit it. Her unwelcomed admirer leaned in closer. "But damn, Baby!" he exclaimed, "I was completely wrong. You're even more beautiful close up. Wow! Where in the hell have you been all of my life?" The intruder glanced around. "And, it appears you're alone. I can't believe that. Why would someone as gorgeous as you be on this beautiful beach—alone?"

A low, throbbing started at the back of Jordan's head and began to move forward.

Then he added, "Hey, I'm not complaining. This could be my good fortune that each of us is here, alone," he gestured with his hands. "This could be to my benefit, huh?" His lips curved into a sly smile. "Yeah, this could just be my lucky day."

Fatigued from lack of sleep, unwanted and unpleasant thoughts of Frank and now this jackass who didn't seem inclined to take a hint combined, Jordan now had the most horrific headache. She closed her eyes and sighed deeply before returning her gaze to him. "Look, whoever you are," she began as pleasantly as she could, "I don't mean to be rude but I'd really just rather be alone."

"Who wants to be alone on a day like today?" he said oblivious to her mood.

"I promise you, you're looking at her."

"I'd like to get to know you," he said in his sexiest voice, trying to melt her down.

He wasn't a bad looking guy, Jordan just wasn't interested in anything he had to say. "I don't think so," she said, trying to douse his flames.

"Really?" he questioned with a stunned look on his face.

"Really." Jordan nodded, giving him a weak smile.

"I was thinking if you play your cards right, I might take you to breakfast now; then we could grab some lunch, and on to dinner later. Wouldn't you like that? You can't pass up an offer like that, can you?"

"That's very kind of you and I appreciate the offer but I'm really not interested." When Jordan saw that he didn't get her message or simply chose to ignore her dismissal, she reached for the sketch and began stuffing her things into her bag and said, "You have a nice day."

"Ahhhh, please don't go." He reached for her hand. "Say yes and stay. Everyone else says no. You don't want to see me beg, do you? Come on, let's do this."

Jordan sighed loudly. After shoving the final items into her bag and was about to get up, she looked up and once again her eyes met with the handsome stranger that she'd seen coming out of the ocean earlier, smiling as he approached them. Her stomach tightened, her heart pounded. There was a sudden stillness, the closer he got. She struggled to will her heart to calm down.

The handsome stranger stopped where the unwanted guest sat and extended his hand, never taking his eyes from Jordan's. "Hi, I'm Tobin Douglas," he said, gripping the man's hand.

"Jeremy Boyd," he answered, grimacing as Tobin held onto his hand a little too tightly, a little too long. Tobin wanted to yank Jeremy Boyd to his feet, but he refrained.

Then, as if responding to Jordan's unspoken displeasure, Tobin winked and asked, "So honey, are you about ready to have some breakfast? After that swim, I'm starved."

Could this lady be more beautiful than when I first saw her? Is that even possible? Tobin silently asked himself. The answer came back to him in a resounding, *yes*! As he took in her beauty; those amazing eyes, luscious bee stung lips that he could kiss and suck non-stop for hours, and a body covered with silky smooth caramel skin that most men would kill to possess. Tobin felt certain that this gorgeous woman was perfectly capable of taking care of herself; still he wanted to look after her. Protect her—at all cost.

Tobin Douglas wasn't sure what was going on inside him, inside his head, his heart; the thumping in his chest as he approached Jordan had been intense, but being near her now, it was hammering out of control, making it difficult to breathe. Even though he didn't think he'd ever stand a chance with a girl like that, here was his golden opportunity to at least give it his best shot. And, he intended to put his heart and soul in his attempt.

Appreciative of Tobin Douglas' intervention, Jordan removed her sunglasses and stared deeply into warm brown eyes that she knew had sent scores of women's hearts aflutter. Her own heart was pounding at an alarming pace.

"Yes sweetheart, I suppose I am." She smiled at him the same way he was smiling at her. Then, she turned her attention to Jeremy Boyd. Tobin turned a cold, hard stare at him too. Jordan knew Jeremy had gotten Tobin's message because the look on his face caused Jeremy to get up quickly from the towel.

"My bad, man. I didn't know she was your lady."

Tobin's face tightened and he snarled, "Yeah, I get that a lot." His lips curled into a brilliant smile but his eyes were of steel.

"See you two around." Jeremy Boyd looked from Jordan to Tobin and said, "You're one lucky brother," he said and hurried away, leaving Jordan and Tobin alone.

"Yeah, I get that a lot too." Tobin glared directly into the Jeremy Boyd's eyes.

"They don't want to leave you alone, do they? Although I can't say that I blame them," Tobin said. He didn't want to appear presumptuous but it would mean everything if the lady was alone on the island.

"Thank you for rescuing me." Jordan broke into his reverie.

"My pleasure. Initially I thought he might be someone special but the look on your face told me otherwise. That definitely wasn't happiness I saw on that beautiful face. Besides," Tobin glanced in the direction of Jeremy Boyd, "he really doesn't look your type."

Jordan wrinkled up her nose. "What do you think is my type?"
"Someone who isn't threatening, or full of himself. Someone who's super nice, caring, passionate, intelligent,

unassuming and he's got to be a real man."

"Any other adjectives you want to throw in there?"

Tobin chuckled deep in his throat. "I could but I think those will suffice for now."

"Would you happen to know such a man?"

Tobin slapped himself across his chest. "That describes me exactly."

Jordan couldn't help smiling at that. Tobin's eyes moved from her beautiful liquid eycs to her luscious baby pink lips and the one thing that dominated his thoughts was what it would be like to kiss those lips.

Tobin Douglas was charming, he exuded confidence and the way he was looking at Jordan, caressing her with his eyes, his voice, she thought it best that she remove herself from this situation because she had no intention of bringing any more complications into her already complicated life.

As she was about to rise up from her towel, Tobin had to stop her. He said, "This is the best time to come out to the beach. It is so peaceful, allow you to communicate with nature." Then drawing his attention from the ocean, he asked, "Are you here alone? Are you married?"

"Yes and no."

Tobin looked at Jordan with raised eyebrows.

She explained further. "Yes, I'm here alone and no, I'm not married."

Her response made Tobin very happy and it showed.

There is that devastating smile again, she thought.

"May I join you in case your gentleman friend decides to come back?"

Jordan looked over to where Jeremy Boyd had wandered off and noticed that he continued to glance at them. "Sure, but that man is no friend of mine. Besides the way you looked at him, I really don't think there's any chance he'll be coming back here."

"Oh, you saw that, huh?"

"I could hardly miss it. That stare was a pretty bold and blatant statement."

"But necessary. Some brothas just don't take no for an answer."

Tobin kneeled on the towel and extended his hand to Jordan. "I really am Tobin Douglas.

"I'm Jordan Banks."

The moment their hands touched, electricity was set off inside her and by the way his hand shook, she was certain he felt it to.

"It's nice to meet you, Jordan Banks."

Jordan eased her hand out of his grip.

Tobin glanced over at Jordan's sketch pad that was partially out of her bag and asked, "May I?"

"Yeah, sure." She reached over, picked up the pad and handed it to him.

He took the pad from her extended hand and after settling down on the towel, he flipped through the pages. "These are yours?"

She nodded her head.

"They are good. Really good."

Her full lips curled into a breathtakingly beautiful smile that revealed dazzling white teeth. "Thank you,"

Tobin raised a hand to his heart as he looked into Jordan's eyes. "There it is."

Jordan's smile faded away and was replaced with a crease in her brow. "What?"

"Well, up until a second ago, a smile covered your face that was earth shattering."

"What are you talking about?"

Damn, she doesn't even know how gorgeous she is, he thought. "I always knew you had one killer smile and I hoped I'd get the opportunity to see it. Even if only for a moment."
Jordan blushed.

Tobin took that opportunity to look at her. Really look at her, at every angle of her feature, every indention, the curves of her face and her mouth that was so ripe for kissing. What he wouldn't give to kiss those lips thoroughly, erase the sadness from her eyes, her life and fill her with joy. Then, trying to erase those thoughts, he asked, "Are you a fashion designer."

"Not really."

"Well, you've got enormous talent should you decide to go that route." Then he changed the subject. "I'm glad that you are here alone."

"And, I'm glad that you rescued me."

"I was almost certain that you were alone because there's no man in his right mind who wouldn't object to someone as gorgeous as you, wearing that awesome suit to come out on beach without him. If he did, he'd need to have his head examined."

Knowing she didn't have anyone who cared that much about her caused her sadness to return. Tobin noticed. "I didn't mean to upset you."

"You have nothing to do with that," she replied and sniffled.

After a moment, he asked, "have you had breakfast?" Before she could respond, he said, "Please, have breakfast with me."
"Food is the last thing on my mind right now."

"It could be just the thing that you need right now."

Jordan didn't respond.

There was a quiet moment between them. Tobin put the sketch pad down. He pulled his legs up against his chest, wrapped his arms around his knees and gave Jordan his full attention. "You want to talk about it?"

"About what?"

"Obviously something is bothering you. I've seen you on the verge of tears twice today so there's gotta be something unpleasant going on. Talk to me," he said sincerely. "I'm a good listener."

She settled back on the towel. "I'm sure you are, but I'm good."

Okay, he thought. *Give it some time.* Then, he asked, "Are you here on vacation?"

"Yes."

"Are you enjoying yourself?"

"I'm trying to make the best of it. What about you?"

"I arrived last night and so far it's been fine. I haven't robbed any banks yet," he added more to bring a smile to her beautiful face than anything, and she didn't disappoint. Her smile lit up her face, making it come to life and his heart took a giant leap.

"I've been here almost a week. I leave tomorrow."

Tobin could barely contain his disappointment at Jordan leaving the island just as they met. Could he persuade her to stay longer? Would she stay longer if he asked? Why would she stay longer if he asked? "I'll be here a week."

"Do you have a family? I mean are you married?" she asked, though she'd already checked out his ring finger on his left hand and noticed that it was void of a ring. Neither was there an indention indicating he'd worn a ring and may have removed it for one reason or another.

"No, I'm a bachelor. And, if you're interested, no, there is no significant other in my life at the moment."

"I really wasn't thinking about that."

"Too much information, right?"

Jordan was surprised that a man such as Tobin wasn't involved with anyone. If that were the case, she was certain that was how he wanted it. She didn't know when she'd seen a man as fine as he. Had she ever seen a man that fine?

"What are you thinking?" He asked, interrupting her thoughts.

Jordan dismissed that question but answered him, saying, "Just surprised at your relationship status."

"Why does that surprise you?"

"Oh, I don't know." Jordan turned down the corners of her lips. "I would have just thought otherwise, that's all."

"Don't get me wrong, I date occasionally and I have as much fun as the next guy, but there's no one special right now."

"I can't believe some lucky woman hasn't snatched you up."

"I supposed I haven't been that fortunate. What about you? Is there someone special in your life?"

Jordan's lips curled down before she answered. "Not anymore."

Tobin noticed the pain on Jordan's face appeared fresh. Whatever happened to her must've occurred recently, too recent to open up right now. Tobin changed the subject but he hoped that they would be able to discuss in the not too distant future what was making her so unhappy, what had caused her so much pain. "Are you a model?"

"A model?" She chuckled. "No. I teach ninth grade Math at Cherokee High School in the great city of Augusta."

"Would you believe Atlanta?"

"You live in Atlanta?"

"We're practically neighbors," he said, feeling good knowing he and Jordan not only lived in America, but in the same state. The gods were looking out for him. "So, you're a teacher. I have a healthy respect for teachers. Both of my parents were teachers."

"Really? What about you, Toby? What do you do?"

"You called me Toby. My mother was the only other person who called me Toby," he said and Jordan thought he almost choked. "I am an oncologist."

"Are you okay?"

"Yeah," he replied, recovering quickly. "I'm fine."

After a moment, Jordan said, "I wouldn't have thought you to be a doctor."

"Why? I don't appear intelligent enough to be a doctor?" He teased.

"No. That wasn't it at all" she said, looking into the face of a man who obviously was older than he looked.

Appearing to read her mind, he said, "I'm thirty-four."

Jordan did a double take. "Are you serious?"

"Cross my heart and hope to die," he said and used his index finger to mark a cross over his heart. "Even if you have set backs, if you stay focused and work hard, they can achieve their goals early and be able to enjoy your career."

Then Jordan remembered something Toby said to earlier. "You said your mother *used to* call you Toby."

"Yeah." He paused a moment. Then, he continued, "My mother died of breast cancer two weeks ago."

"I'm sorry to hear that. How are you?

"As good as I can be I guess. Anyway, I'm dealing with it. She was a wonderfully caring and compassionate woman. She is the reason that I chose oncology as my profession. My mother was diagnosed with cancer eight years ago and for years, I watched her suffer as she battled the illness; going through the treatments; chemo, radiation, sickness taking its toll on the patient, the family." He shook his head as sadness engraved his face. "When it was over, I was devastated but in a way, relieved for her and myself because she didn't have to suffer anymore." Toby looked out briefly across the ocean. Jordan remained quiet. What she wanted to do most was reach out and touch his hand, his pain-filled face, assure him that it was all right to be sad when we lose someone dear to us, it was all right to be devastated over that loss and also to move forward, but she refrained. How could she tell him how to face his grief when she was faced with a challenge that was far more insignificant yet she wasn't realistically able to move forward? Then Toby asked, "Do you have close family ties?"

Jordan found that she was beginning to feel comfortable talking with Toby and she shared some of her family history with him; twin siblings who are younger than she. She didn't mention they never knew the twins' father or that her father was an Italian businessman who was visiting the country, met her mother and when he left town, he left Jordan's mother pregnant with her, but she did mentioned that eleven years ago, they lost her mother to a drug overdose and since that time, Jordan has taken care of herself and the twins. After graduating from Clark Atlanta University, with a Math major, she became a teacher and that immediate salary met their immediate needs, allowing her make sure the twins received an education as well. Paying back student loans and assisting her siblings hadn't left a hefty bank account at her disposal.

Jordan said, "But as long as I can remember, I've wanted to be a designer and design fabulous clothes but Augusta isn't the ideal city to launch a career as a fashion designer."

"I commend you for making the sacrifice of taking care of your siblings."

"I didn't do it alone. Mrs. Irene, our neighbor who was my mom's best friend, helped a lot, but I loved looking after the twins," Jordan said as if it was the most natural thing in the world.

"I'm sure, but taking on the challenges of two younger people, and ensuring they get the education necessary to grow into productive citizens; was quite an undertaking and it appears you fulfilled your promise to your mother," he said then asked, "but when are you going to pursue your dream?"

"That's another conversation," she said and Toby could tell that that was something she didn't want to talk about at that time. They fell into a temporary silence, staring at each other. Toby couldn't help thinking that Jordan was the most gorgeous woman he'd ever seen, with the most incredible eyes. And, he could tell they are for real. Not that he has anything against sistas who wore the colored contacts to flavor up their eyes, but hers were real and they were gorgeous.

Toby broke their silence. "Why don't we get that breakfast? I really am starved."

Jordan continued to stare at him for a moment, then said, "Okay."

Toby assisted in putting her things back into her handbag. She noticed his strong hands and clean nails. He was even more gorgeous than when she first saw him emerging out of the ocean. "I've got to run back to the hotel and change."

"So do I. Where are you staying?"

"The Wexler," she replied, pointing toward the hotel that was in walking distance from the ocean.

"A little further down," he said.

Toby walked with her to her hotel. Does she have bowed legs, he wondered, not wanting to be too obvious and stare at her legs. He'd always had a weakness for a woman with beautiful bowed legs.

"I'll meet you at your hotel in a few."

"Okay."

CHAPTER 3

Jordan entered the lobby of the quaint and alluring atmosphere of the picturesque, tropical surroundings of the 60 room Wexler Hotel. Guests were coming and going through the lobby that housed wicker furniture, tables, lamps, large framed prints and modern art pieces on the walls and colorful tropical plants.

The lobby buzzed with excitement as she made her way through the guests on her way to her room that was pale yellow and had a lovely view of the island's exotic splendor; blue, rippling waters, beautiful white sand beaches and glorious palm trees swaying in the gentle breezes.

It was a comfortable room that was equipped with modern furniture; a queen size bed with a pale yellow comforter, several floral pillows, a sofa, chairs, nightstands and lamps. The carpet was a floral print that went well with the walls and furniture.

Jordan removed her swimsuit and took a quick shower. She brushed on a little makeup and nude lip gloss. After putting on white Capri pants, a white and pink blouse and sticking her feet into white wedged sandals, she grabbed a white wicker purse from the dresser and dashed out the door to meet Toby.

Jordan exited the elevator and saw Toby standing near the registration desk. She liked everything about the man; the way he looked, his broad chest under the white short sleeve pullover, tan shorts that hugged his taut hips, short black hair with a natural curl and sideburns that faded into a full short cut beard. Jordan knew she'd never seen anyone as handsome as Tobin Douglas in her entire life.

Seeing her approaching him, his eyes twinkled, his stomach did flip flops and his heart beat savagely against his chest. When he smiled, his lips curled back over dazzling white teeth. He watched as she gracefully crossed the lobby; her long, slightly curled hair flowing over her shoulders, the curves of her body as she moved, her smooth beautiful skin. She looked amazing. He couldn't help but imagine those legs wrapped tightly around him, holding him like a vice against her beautiful body and never letting him go. He could handle that, for an entire lifetime.

Toby shook his head to clear his thoughts as he walked towards her.

She slipped her purse strap over her shoulder, walked up and as she reached for his extended hands, she noticed the scent of the expensive cologne he was wearing. "Hello," she greeted him.

"Hi." He took her hands into his a brief moment before she pulled them away. "You look fantastic." Toby allowed his eyes to move down her body as respectfully as he could.

"So do you," she replied looking up into the eyes of a man who was at least eight inches taller than her five seven frame. "So where are we off to?"

"What would you like to eat?"

"Oh, I don't know. Surprise me."

With that, they left her hotel and walked out onto the street. Toby hailed a taxi.

"I thought we'd eat at one of the restaurants in the area," Jordan commented.

"You asked me to surprise you, remember? So that's what I'm gonna do. But, we're not going very far."

She smiled her approval. The taxi pulled to a stop in front of them, they got in and Toby spouted off directions to their destination. Within minutes, they pulled up to one of the most fabulous hotels on the island. He paid the driver, then they entered the lobby of the Ritz-Carlton Golf & Spa that was elegant luxury from the sparkling crystal chandelier hanging from the ceiling, plush sofas and chairs, beautiful bouquets of tropical flowers and palm plants to the beautiful artwork that adorned the cream colored walls.

They walked down the long carpeted foyer to double doors that led to the hotel's signature restaurant, before they entered the semi-crowded room and after being seated immediately, a waitress brought water and menus that she placed on the table and left, giving them time to decide what they wanted for breakfast. They scanned the breakfast list.

"See anything interesting?" he asked.

"I like grits. I don't see any grits, eggs or bacon on this menu," she said.

"You can order it if you'd like but you're on this beautiful island, why not live dangerously?" he teased.

She looked up and seeing the humorous look on his face, she smiled and said, "I'll have what you're going to have. Then, setting her menu aside, Jordan folded her hands in front of her.
"Okay, then," he said as the waitress reappeared.

"I think each of us will have a tropical fruit salad with hot citrus syrup, baked plantain, coconut bake, carrot juice and coffee."

"Very good, Sir," the waitress said, smiled and left the table.

"So, what are you doing on this beautiful, romantic island alone? As soon as the question left his mouth, Toby was sorry he asked seeing sadness crossed her beautiful face. He tried to distract her by pointing to something inconsequential out the window. "That's a beautiful sailboat, don't you think. I'm thinking that I might buy one," he smiled at her.

The waitress returned with the food and before she left their table, said, "I hope you and your guest enjoy your meal, Mr. Douglas."

"You eat here often?"

"Actually, I do."

"This looks wonderful."

"It tastes even better."

Jordan began to fork some food into her mouth. "Oooh, this is good." She rolled the food around in her mouth, savoring it.

"I knew you would like it."

She ran her tongue over her lips to get the extra syrup. Toby felt an ache in the lower part of his stomach, at the mesmerizing sight of her tongue gliding along her lips and only wished he could lick those lips whether there was syrup on them or not.

Each time she packed fruit salad with hot syrup into her mouth, she closed her eyes and chewed slowly and Toby could hardly eat his food for watching her.

After finishing breakfast, Jordan put her fork down and wiped her mouth with the colorful linen napkin. "That was so good."

"I'm glad you enjoyed it," Toby said, wiped his mouth and asked, "What would you like to do today?"

Jordan's head snapped up. "Well, I don't know, but I do know what I want for breakfast in the morning."

They chuckled. Toby loved the sound of her laughter.

After a moment, Toby asked, "How do you feel about carnivals?"

"Carnivals?" Her eyes lit up. "I love carnivals."

"There's one not far from here. Are you game?"

"Hell yeah."

"We can enjoy a few rides and enjoy ourselves."

"We'll have to hold off on the rides for a while. You know what will happen if we get on rides with a full stomach."

"Yeah," he chuckled. "We'd probably barf all over everyone near us."

Jordan couldn't help laughing at his joke and he couldn't be happier seeing her smile again.

After Toby paid the ticket, they left the restaurant and took a taxi the short distance to the carnival grounds. Walking around, their eyes swept past numerous activities, they made purchases and they enjoyed performers dancing in their traditional costumes. They applauded loudly to the well rehearsed youth choirs that sang, dropped a few bucks in an elderly man's hat as he sat on the ground, playing lively tunes on his guitar, and they marveled at wood carvers as they plied their trade into regal, exquisite statues.

Jordan and Toby walked past kiddie rides and witnessed happy, contented mothers in groups on the sidelines watching their children have fun.

After a while, Toby asked, "Are you having fun yet?"

"Uh huh. This is nice."

"How big are you on roller coasters?"

"I don't know," Jordan answered, remembering a bad experience she and her sister, Steffie, had on a roller coaster when she was a pre-teen. The wind and speed of the ride nearly pulled her little sister out of the seat.

Jordan had wrapped one arm around Steffie and gripped the bar to the gate with her other hand until the ride was over.

"Chicken," he teased.

She'd vowed to never get on a roller coaster again. And, she hadn't. It looked as though that was about to change. "Did you just call me chicken? You didn't just call me chicken, did you?"

"I believe I did."

"Come on. Let's do this."

Jordan grabbed Toby's hand and begun to run toward the ride, pulling him along. After getting their tickets, they got into their seat and the attendants secured their gate. The machine squeaked and jerked as it moved slowly down the track, but within minutes, the snakelike machine was moving at record breaking speed. When the speed increased, Jordan began screaming and had fallen hard against Toby's chest and he wrapped his arms tightly around her. Screams could be heard all around them.

When the roller coaster came to a stop and the attendant unlatched their gate, Jordan sprung out of her seat and ran away from the ride.

"Wasn't that fun?" Toby chuckled, catching up to her.

"Yeah, right," she replied giving him a dark eye.

"Come on, you know you enjoyed it. What should we tackle next? Something daring; speed, excitement."

"I believe I can do just fine without any more speed and excitement," Jordan said.

"Ahhhh, where is your sense of adventure; having fun, living on the edge?"

"Get outta here," Jordan teased tugging at his arm.

They decided to walk around some more before tackling another ride.

Toby asked, "Want to play some games? Or, are you afraid that I'll beat up on you?"

"Are you serious?" Jordan was ready and willing to accept that challenge. "You're on, my friend. Which game would you like to play first?"

"Doesn't matter. I'm gonna whip the pants off you." He gave her a sly smile.

"Bring it." She returned a sly smile.

They played a number of games, they won stuffed animals and just as Jordan was about to secure another win, Toby said, "Ahhhh, no fair."

"What are you crying about now? You're such a baby." Then she squealed in delight, "See, I've got the juice. How many games have you won?"

"Let me see." Toby lifted his hand to count his fingers. "Aaaah, none. Oh wait. What about the apple bobbing contest? I won that one fair and square because you were too chicken hearted to bob for the apple." He chuckled.

"Did you get a good look at the guy who bobbed ahead of us? That brother looked like he hadn't trimmed his beard or washed his face in at least a year," Jordan chuckled.

"Come to think of it, he did look a little rough around the edges, huh?" Toby looked over to her and they laughed. "Are you ready to go on another ride?"

"Yes, the Ferris wheel," Jordan suggested.

"Allll riigghht."

"Let's get a cotton candy first," Jordan said with her arms stuffed with her winnings.

"You like cotton candy, too?"

"I sure do. A little sugar ain't gonna hurt us."

"Who's gonna care if all our teeth are rotted out by the time we reach fifty?"

"Speak for yourself," Jordan said as they rushed up to the stand where Jordan purchased two sticks of cotton candy and handed one to Toby. He took a huge bite out of his as did Jordan.

As they made their way to the Ferris wheel stand, Jordan gave a small child one of the stuffed animals that she won. They bought tickets that they presented to the attendant who secured their safety locks and within a short time, the Ferris wheel had filled up and the ride began.

"You will protect me, won't you?" Toby teased, looking over at Jordan.

"Absolutely, I will." She looked at him and her gaze warmed his heart.

Soon the giant Ferris wheel began to move and they ascended slowly. Then, picking up speed, soon it was moving rapidly. Jordan began to scream and the next thing Toby knew, she was in his arm, burying her face in his chest and holding on to him with him smiling, pleased that she was in his arms again.

He leaned in closer and with his lips against her ear, he whispered, "Don't worry, I'll protect you."

As she was about to whisper in his ear, he turned and their lips nearly touched. Jordan quickly pulled her lips away. She knew that had she kissed him, it would never have ended with just one kiss.

The wheel rushed around several more times, then, it began to slow down. Jordan and Toby looked at each other, a puzzled expression on their faces.

"Is the ride over?" Jordan asked, moving out of the comfort of Toby's arms.

"It can't be. We've only been riding a few minutes," he replied.

Then the Ferris Wheel came to a complete stop.

"I ain't believing this," Toby said, then leaned over the side and called down to the operator, "Hey buddy, what's going on with the ride?"

"Mister, we just got on this thing. Come on, get this thing moving. Our time isn't over yet. You're ripping us off," Jordan said.

When Jordan turned and looked at Toby, he was laughing so hard it was difficult for him to speak. Finally, between chuckles he said, "Yeah, buddy, let's get this thing moving." He laughed some more.

Nothing happened. Then, other riders began yelling down at the equipment operator.

Then, an announcer came out from the operator's booth. "Ladies and gentlemen," he began, his voice booming, "we apologize for the inconvenience, but we're currently experiencing some technical difficulties with the equipment."

A number of gasps and groans could be heard from other passengers.

"Don't worry," the announcer continued. "We're working on the problems and will have the ride up and running as soon as possible."

A rash of verbal insults and profanity were directed at the announcer.

Jordan looked around and it suddenly dawned on her where they were positioned on the Ferris Wheel. "Oh crap, did you know that we're one seat away from the top of this thing?"

"Does it make you feel less safe because we're higher in the air?" He snickered.

With that, Jordan elbowed him in his ribs.

"Ouch," he exclaimed loudly, pretending the jab hurt. "I wouldn't be surprised if you broke a few of my ribs."

She turned to him and playfully, slapped him several times on his arm.

"Help! Help me somebody! This lady is trying to kill me!"

They chuckled together. After a moment, they settled back in their seats and waited for repairs to be made to the equipment.

"So Miss Jordan Banks, you are a Math teacher who wants to be a fashion designer?"

"Yes."

"There's absolutely nothing wrong with being a teacher. It takes a special kind of person to be a teacher. I think other than being a parent, teaching is one of the best profession one can hope to have, not to mention one of the most difficult jobs, but your desire to be a fashion designer doesn't surprise me. It's obvious from your sketches that you have a flare for it. You're a real talent."

Jordan accepted the compliment. "Thank you. That's all I've ever wanted to do but Augusta is not exactly the city that calls out to fashion designers."

"Ever thought about moving to another city? There are many other cities that would welcome good fashion designers."

"I know," Jordan said wistfully.

"Is there any reason why you haven't made the move?"

Jordan didn't want to pursue that conversation further. She turned to Toby. "When I came here, all I wanted to do was enjoy some foreign cuisine, have a glass of wine, maybe two, who's counting, relax and think about what I want to do with my life. I intend to use this time to forget my troubles, reclaim my life and move forward."

"You can do that. You are the kind of woman who can do anything you want."

"I wish it was that simple," she said and when he saw the renewed pain etched in her face, Toby wondered who had hurt her so deeply because what he was looking at was pain that only time could heal. Then suddenly, her smile returned and she changed the subject, "I really wish I lived in the right city to push my designs."

"Move."

"I don't think so."

"Why not?"

"I can't move."

"Why not?"

"My home is in Augusta, my job, a place for Steffie and Steven to come home, and I have an elderly neighbor, Mrs. Irene, who lives across the street and I care a lot about."

"Steffie and Steven are adults, college graduates. I'm not saying desert your family. All I'm asking is when are you going to start thinking about Jordan? When are you going to start looking out for yourself, have the kind of life that you want?"

There was enormous admiration in Toby's eyes when he said, "You're a beautiful woman on the outside and my instincts tells me you're just as beautiful inside, that most of your life you've made sacrifices, done your share of looking after others and it appears that it's time you did something totally selfish for a change. Do something for Jordan. Something for you." He used his index finger to gently punch her in her chest. "Do you, Jordan. Do you."

Her eyes went down to his finger.

Toby continued. "I'm sure everyone wants the same for you. Why don't you think about starting your own business? Create your fashion line. You could even market it on the internet. You know there is so much you can do on the internet now. And, there are other options."

"And, turn my home into a business? I don't think so. It's not that easy to give up everything and start fresh."

"Why? People do it all the time. You're smart, energetic and you're young. People a lot older than you have turned their lives upside down to get what they want. That is called realizing your dream, living your best life." He paused, then said, "You know, Jordan, if you're satisfied with the status quo, then that's fine, but if you want something different, do it, but don't come up with excuses that aren't valid."

"I'm not coming up with excuses. Toby," she began, but stopped suddenly, noticing the change that came across his face as he stared at her. "What's wrong?"

"I was just trying to decide whether I want to swim around in those eyes the rest of the day or kiss those lips until they bleed."

"What?" Jordan said, a furrow in her brow.

"I'm sorry. I got carried away for a moment. Please forgive me," he teased. "I promise to be a good boy from now on, okay?"

She gave him a sidelong glance.

"I promise." He lifted his right hand. "I'm gonna be on my best behavior the rest of the day."

She glanced at him, then looked away.

"Why not move to a larger city? The opportunities are greater. I don't have to tell you that."

"I know that but…"

"Just make a decision and go for it. Atlanta, for instance. You could have enormous success in the A-T-L."

"You really think so?"

"I absolutely do."

"Is everything in your life that simple?"

"Nothing in my life is simple. I just try to make the best of what's in front of me."

"Do you always get it right?"

"No, sometimes I get it wrong, and when I do, I try again. You don't let one wrong decision defeat you."

"I've made some decisions in my life that have come back and bitten me." Jordan paused a moment and stared out across the carnival grounds.

"I was involved with a man for three years until a week ago."

He sat quietly listening, but when she hesitated, he decided he could approach the subject that he'd been wanting to from the time he laid eyes on her on the beach earlier. "You were crying on the beach this morning. Did it have anything to do with the man you were involved with?"

"Everything." She tugged at her earlobe. "I was in my feelings because of an obvious bad decision that I made. Simply, I chose the wrong man." Jordan found that she had begun to relax and felt comfortable enough to share even more of her life with him.

"What went wrong?"

She exhaled deeply, "I fell in love."

He lifted her chin with his fingertips and gently guided her face back towards his. "Falling in love is never wrong," he said, softly.

"It was in my case." She sniffed and returned her gaze to the ocean. "I was very much in love with him. We were together one night, he left my house the following day, and he married someone else that same day. He erased my self esteem, he hurt and humiliated me more than you could imagine." Tears began to trickle down her cheek.

He reached up to brush away her tears. Her abrupt movement left his fingertips suspended in the air. "You didn't do anything wrong. You fell in love with a man who was wrong for you. Falling in love with that man was a gift for him only he wasn't man enough to realize it." After a moment,

Toby said, "This too shall pass. Just don't lose yourself in this situation."

"This is very painful not to mention embarrassing."

"Don't be embarrassed. You fell in love with a dick who obviously didn't appreciate what he had. I don't mean to get all up in your personal business but you will find that I am the least judgmental person you could ever know."

"His name is Frank! Frank Benjamin! When I met Frank, he quickly became my heart, my soul mate. He was everything to me, and I loved him unconditionally. He was everything I wanted in a man—or so I thought."

Toby didn't say anything. But he gave her an encouraging look to continue.

"As it turned out, he didn't really love me after all. How stupid could I have been? Why didn't I know? Why didn't I see it coming? I have been such a fool."

"You are nobody's fool. I happen to think you are a pretty great lady."

"No?" She laughed bitterly. "Then, why would he do this to me?" Jordan had said far more than she intended to say but once the words started tumbling out, they didn't want to stop.

Toby stared at her in shock. "Are you kidding me?"

"Does it look like I'm kidding you? He had all these plans for his life but I wasn't included. I learned of his deception in a phone call from his mother." She began to cry.

Toby's mind began to race. How could he help Jordan? What could he say to her? He placed his arms around her, held her close as she continued to cry.

"Let it out, baby. Let it all out. Sometimes the best way to deal with the hurt is to just allow it to happen. Allow yourself to hurt, allow you to be sad. Give yourself permission to do exactly what you need to do until all the hurt, pain, disappointment is gone."

"How am I ever gonna get over something like this?"

"Time. Let time take you through the pain."

After a while, Jordan pushed away from Toby, wiping away her tears with her hand. "I just don't understand how he could do this."

"Because he's an ass, sweetie."

"Why didn't I see what was happening? I'm not a stupid person. By most standards, I'm pretty smart. I've got really good gut instincts, good intuition, but this, this came right out of left field. I saw this man almost every night. Why didn't I see it coming?" Jordan trembled staring off into the distance but seeing nothing as new sobs escaped her.

"Your life doesn't stop because someone else's plans changes, and you can't change people. You can only change your reaction to them. So what you have to do is move towards something that is important to you. This situation is unfortunate, but it doesn't stop you from living. Allow yourself to be sad—until the healing begins. When you need to cry, cry. Let the toxins out so that you can feel again, live again, and eventually love again. It takes guts but you will get there." He paused a moment to allow her to digest it. Then he said, "You can't continue to live until you get past the waste, put it in the garbage where it belongs. Give yourself permission to believe that life goes on and most importantly, give yourself permission to live again. Better days are coming and that could just be tomorrow." He continued to hold her and talked with her. "He threw away what I am sure was the best thing that will ever happen to him in his miserable lifetime." Toby continued to rock Jordan. You don't have to forget him. Most of us don't forget the people who come into our lives and leave a significant mark. Remember him. Remember the lousy son of a bitch that he is. Just don't attach any importance to him."

Toby rocked Jordan from side to side and he continued to hold her and talked to her until she stopped crying. "I just wish you didn't love him so much."

"I wish I didn't either."

"We're talking about three, almost four years. How can I remember him and not attach any importance to it?

"Easily." He reached into his pants pocket and pulled out a clean white handkerchief and gently wiped away her tears before handing it to her.

She accepted the handkerchief. "Thank you. You must think I'm a wimp, crying because of a man."

"No I don't. That was a very human response to a very ugly and difficult situation." Toby was thoughtful a moment before saying softly, "It's a good thing to be able to cry. I haven't cried since I was a boy. My mother always thought it wasn't a good thing for a man to cry. I didn't even cry when my father died."

"Didn't you want to cry?"

"I was really young when my dad died so I probably didn't know or understand the loss. But when my mother died, now that was real. I've never hurt so much about anything in my life before and as much as I wanted to cry, I didn't but that's another story. Anyway, you didn't see anything wrong with your relationship with that guy because you knew where your heart and mind were and you expected the same from him. You loved him. It's that simple and no one can fault you for it."

"Are you sure you are not a therapist?" Jordan chuckled a little.

"You have such a sense of people. You seem to have harnessed a real grasp on human emotions.

Wiping her nose, she said, "I've monopolized all your time with my tears and my pity party. Now, I want to hear about you."

Toby talked freely about his school years; the sports he'd played, how he attended Harvard Law School which he gave up after two years and switched his focus to medicine after his mother was diagnosed with cancer.

"It's incredible getting to know you like this." He didn't care that the ride wasn't repaired. He was just happy that Jordan appeared to be feeling better.

"May I ask you something personal?"

"Of course, anything."

"Why isn't there someone special in your life? No, forget that. Let me ask you this? What do you look for in a woman? What would be your ideal woman?"

"Someone who is pretty, kind, resourceful, intelligent, funny, a good listener, a good conversationalist, sensitive."

"Is that all?" she said, smiling.

"I don't ask for much," he teased.

"What's the first thing that attracts you most about a woman?"

"Well, like most men, the physical is right up there but what really attracts me is her mind. That is what keeps me interested in her. I like a woman who can think on her feet. You? What kind of man appeals to you and don't tell me the stupid ones because I wouldn't believe you." He chuckled.

"I really don't know anymore. But right now, I'm completely off the market, so it really doesn't matter."

"Now, that's not what us good guys want to hear."

"Sometimes it hurts too much."

"But sometimes the hurt is so good that it's worth it to give it one more try."

"That doesn't make any sense."

"Surc it does."

Jordan looked at Toby and sees the look on his face. "You are so bad."

"I just see that lame brain for who he is without the benefit of even knowing him but his actions doesn't speak for the rest of us. That guy needs his ass whipped."

"Are you saying you would fight for my honor?" She teased.

"You bet I would. That cat is not ready for this jungle."

Jordan gave him a dark look. "What happened doesn't say a lot about my judgment either."

"I'd never condemn anyone who trusted and believed in someone and thought they wouldn't receive the same in return."

"How is it that you are so sweet and understanding?"

"I know this is a tough situation and I hate to see you go through this. If I could reach into your chest with both hands and hold your heart in these hands," he said while holding his hands outstretched, palms up, "I would comfort it, protect it so guys like that ass hole can't get anywhere near it. I would give anything to protect your heart—protect you."

"You don't even know me. I could be some sort of Jezebel."

"But you are not and I do know that."

Just then, it began to rain.

"What?" Jordan said, looking up as rain drops washed over her face and down her clothes. "I don't believe this. We're gonna get soaked."

Immediately Toby began to remove his shirt and draped it over her head.

"Chivalry is alive and well." Jordan lifted the shirt so that it covered his head as well. "You are so sweet. Thank you, again."

"For what?"

"For your kindness. Everything. It appears that I'm going to spend my last vacation day thanking you."

"Then I'm encouraged."

"You are?"

"Well yeah. That tells me you're looking ahead and that you will be spending your vacation with me."

"You do remember that I will be leaving the island tomorrow?"

"Perhaps I can talk you into staying a few extra days."

"I don't think so." She smiled weakly.

Toby looked wistfully at her.

As sudden as the rain had started, it had stopped and the sun was shining again. Jordan lifted the shirt off both their heads, held it up and looked sheepishly at Toby. "It's all wet."

"It's just a little damp."

"Let's hang it across this bar. It'll be dry in no time." Jordan spread the shirt out along the gate to their seat, then she looked at him and the smile she gave him was bright enough to destroy any blizzard.

Toby smiled looking at Jordan and said, "Hi."

"Hi," she replied and they chuckled together.

CHAPTER 4

It was a warm day; the mid-afternoon sky was once again blue and cloudless. Jordan wiped her hand across her forehead to remove the sweat beads.

"We've been up here more than an hour, we've gotten wet, we're now dry and it's getting kind of hot. I wonder when are they going to get this thing fixed?" Then, she begun to playfully drum her fists on the bar to their seat and she started chanting, "Fix this ride, fix this ride, fix this ride." Before long not only did Toby join in, but the couple above them and the one beneath them did as well.

The chanting went on for a while with a chorus of chants going around the entire Ferris wheel. Then, Toby looked up toward the couple in the seat above them, and called out, "Hello up there. You guys doing okay?"

"What happening, man?" a male voice returned.

"How is the weather in your part of the world?" Toby continued.

"It's hot as hell where we are. What about down there where you guys are?"

"Yeah, we're roasting like potatoes in this giant screw up and my lady is pissed off that she's about ready to commit homicide on someone," Toby said looking directly into Jordan's eyes. "She's gotten a serious tan and is even more gorgeous than anyone I've ever seen, but she's still pissed off. She's missing out on her ride. I keep telling her that she's gonna get her full ride, but you know how women are."

Jordan gently elbowed Toby in his ribs again.

"Ooowww," he screeched.

"Shut your mouth," she whispered, placing a hand over his mouth. "You're such a baby."

He allowed his head to drop on her shoulder, pretending to be in pain. "You're trying to kill me."

"Hey, what's going on down there?" the gentleman from the seat above asked, looking down at Jordan and Toby.

"This woman is trying to kill me, man," Toby replied.

"Are you two having a lovers' quarrel in mid air?" the man asked, jokingly.

"Naaaaw. We're fine," Jordan said, then to Toby with a finger to her lips, "Shhhh."

"You expect me to be quiet when you just broke several of my ribs?" he asked, loudly.

"I did not," Jordan protested.

"Did too," he continued to tease her.

"What are you guys up to?" the gentleman from the chair below called up to them. "You guys are having entirely too much fun. Tell us what's happening so we can join in."

"My lady just took out a rib or two for no reason," Toby said, out loud.

"That's abuse, man. Aren't you gonna sue the pants off of her….Ouch," the man in the chair at the top said. "My woman just belted the hell out of me."

"And, he deserved it," the woman accompanying him said.

"What's going on with these women today, man? It must be something in the air because they are pretty feisty," Toby said, a devilish grin on his handsome face.

"You think they're mad because the rain came and their hair got all wet?" the man below asked.

"You know they don't like it when their hair gets messed up," Toby said.

"You're telling me," the man above them said.

"Maybe they arc just hot or hungry," Toby put in.

"Or both," the man above replied.

All the while Jordan sat with her arms folded across her chest and gave Toby a side eye. He noticed and asked, grinning, "What? You're not gonna whack me again, are you?" Toby playful shielded his chest against another blow from Jordan.

"I haven't decided yet."

"Hey guys, I need help. My lady is about to use me as her punching bag again," Toby informed the others.

"He's lying," Jordan said.

Leaning over his seat to look down at the couple below them, Toby asked, "You don't have a fighting woman too, do you?"

"Yeah man, this woman just whacked me up side my head," the man below them said.

"You can't believe a word he says," the woman with him replied.

"Hey guys, since we are all in this together, why don't we introduce ourselves. I'm Tobin and this is Jordan."

The man above them said, looking down toward the other two couples, "I'm Jim and this is my wife, Trish."

Then the man from the seat below them said, "I'm Martin and this is Gina."

"Glad to meet all of you," Toby said.

The three couples waved to each other.

"Hello, down there," Martin yelled down to the Ferris wheel operator.

"What about getting some food up here to us? We're starved."

"How is he going to do that?" Gina giggled. "Do you think the man has wings?"

That brought a roar of laughter from the couples.

Jordan had eaten more at breakfast that morning than she had since her breakup with Frank. Now that she felt like eating again, she had become ravenous. "Yeah," she yelled down. "Send up a couple of sandwiches and some cold drinks."

"I'm with you, Jordan," Martin commented.

Gina followed that with, "Some dessert would be nice also."

They all laughed.

"Yeah," Jim chimed in, "and a pitcher of martinis.

"I'll take some curry goat," Trish said, chuckling.

"Ugh," Gina and Jordan said in unison.

"What's wrong with curry goat?" Trish asked.

Giggling, Jordan said, "Oh, nothing."

"I saw that," Trish joked, catching the humorous looks between Jordan and Gina.

Then, running her fingers through limp, damp hair, Gina said, "I've got to do something about this hair."

"What wrong with your hair?" Trish asked, looking down at Gina.

"It's wet and looks a mess. I don't have that wash and wear kind of hair that the two of you have," she said, referring to Trish and Jordan.

"Your hair looks fine to me," Jordan said.

"You think so?" Gina, the pretty black woman chuckled.

"Yeah, it looks fine," Jordan said.

"Where is the food?" Gina said. "This is too much. I'm hot, thirsty and I'm hungry."

"I'm with you, Gina," Toby yelled down to her.

Suddenly, the Ferris wheel made a loud horrible screeching sound then it began to move slowly, then picking up speed until it was rotating again and again with everyone cheering the success of the equipment being operational again.

After a while, the ride began to slow down, then it came to a complete stop and the riders got off. As soon as the three couples were on the ground, Toby caught Jordan's hand and pulled her over to the other two couples whose ages were late twenties, early thirties.

The women hugged each other and the men shook hands as if they were long-time friends.

"Wasn't it horrifying being stuck up there like that?" Trish said, her blue eyes sparking with exasperation.

"I thought it was kinda hot," Gina, the mocha skin beauty with dark, exotic eyes, replied.

"It was a little uncomfortable for me," Jordan said.

"I've got to find a nail salon to have my nails repaired," Trish said. "I was scared shitless up there. When that thing stopped, I gripped that bar so tightly that several of my nails broke."

Then, touching Gina's hair, Jordan said to her, "See, I told you. There's nothing wrong with your hair. It looks great."

Gina reached into her purse, removed her compact and checked her hair. The rain had caused her previously silky curls to frizz. Then, she said to Jordan, "I love your outfit. That's an unusual blouse. You didn't happen to get it from the island, did you?"

"I made it," Jordan replied, easing her hand out of Toby's.

"Did you really?" Trish said, catching Jordan by her shoulders and turned her around to get a look at the entire outfit. "This is exquisite."
"It certainly is," Gina agreed.

"Thanks," Jordan accepted the compliment from both women."

"Jordan," Gina began, "girl, you are stunning." She then looked at Toby and said, "I bet all these island boys are trying to get at your lady, huh?"

"They certainly have been. I had to run some guy away from her a little while ago. I mean the brotha didn't want to take no for an answer," Toby answered.

"Do you and Toby have children?" Trish asked, looking from Jordan to Toby who was grinning from ear to ear.

"Not yet," Toby teased, looking at Jordan.

"He's joking," Jordan answered. "We're not married. As a matter of fact, Toby and I just met this morning."

"Really?" Gina said in surprise. "You two seem so in sync."
Toby gave Jordan a smile.

Trish looked at her watch and suggested, "Why don't we get something to eat?"

"That sounds great," Jordan agreed.

Trish said, "Why don't we go to The Montego Caribbean Cuisine. They have the best curry food on the island."

"Let's go get the woman some goat," Toby said and they all chuckled.

On the street, the couples walked along the street, getting to know each other better when suddenly a little girl, about four years old, ran up to Jordan, threw her arms around her legs and squeeze them. Jordan kneeled down to the little dark complexion cutie with huge hazel eyes and two long sandy braids trailing down her back.

"Hello there. How are you?" Jordan asked her.

"Fine," the little girl replied, admiring the stuffed animals Jordan was carrying in her arms, while Toby carried a largest one.

"Will you hold these for me while I tie your shoe laces?" Jordan said, handing the little girl the stuffed bears. "Let's get these tied so you don't trip, okay."

"Okay." The little girl's eyes lit up as she took the teddy bears from Jordan's outstretched hands.

As Jordan tied the laces, she asked, "What's your name?"

"Kendal."

"Kendal? That's a very pretty name. My name is Jordan."

"Your name is pretty too, Miss Jordan. And, you are pretty."

"Thank you. I think you are pretty also. There, all done." Jordan stood up and took the teddy bears from the little girl's hands. "Where is your mom?"

"She's over there." The girl pointed toward a tall, thin and pretty chocolate colored woman with braids wrapped around her head and carrying a bag in her hand.

"I like your teddy bears too," the little girl said.

"You do?"

"Yes."

"Well, you know what. I've been carrying these teddy bears around all day, I'm very tired of carrying them both and I'm looking for someone to help me take care of one of them. Do you know anyone who would take care of one of them for me?"

"Yes! Me! I'll take care of him for you," the little girl said excitedly.

"Which one would you like?"

The little girl selected a teddy bear and Jordan handed it to her. She hugged the bear against her chest. "Thank you."

"You're welcome. Now may I have a hug?"

"Yes." The little girl wrapped a long thin arm around Jordan's neck and squeezed tightly. "Goodbye, pretty lady."

Jordan waved to the little girl who turned and ran off to the woman waiting nearby.

Jim hailed a taxi. All six of them piled in, Martin gave directions to the restaurant and they rode the eight blocks. When they arrived, the men argued in good humor who would pay the fare, they exited the taxi and headed towards the restaurant.

The restaurant was nearly crowded but after a few minutes, they were seated. Toby slid into a seat next to Jordan, and they placed their orders that ranged from curry goat, jerk chicken, jerk rib eye steaks, tilapia, white rice with red kidney beans and coconut milk, red garlic potatoes, to Caribbean slaw, fried ripe plantain, stir fried vegetables. While they ate, they learned more about each other; Trish and Jim, both attorneys from Philadelphia, Martin was a computer engineer and Gina, a New York realtor. Jordan and Toby shared their professions as well.

"Jordan is a Math teacher with aspirations of being a fashion designer," Toby informed the group.

Gina was quick to say to Jordan, "Your desire to become a fashion designer doesn't surprise me at all. You did an amazing job on that outfit you're wearing. It's kick ass."

Trish dabbed her mouth with her napkin. "You really should look into the fashion business. You're such a talent. Girl, do it. Life is too short to wait for all those tomorrows to go by then you wished you'd done something yesterday. Here, taste a piece of this. It is divine," she said of a piece of curry goat she cut off with her knife.

"I don't think so." Jordan squinted up her face and gave Gina a look.

"I saw that," Trish said, chuckling.

Jordan and Gina snickered.

"My tilapia is just fine, thank you very much," Jordan said. "Would you like to sample my fish?"

"I don't mind if I do," Trish said and used her knife to cut off a piece of Jordan's tilapia. "Hmmm good," she acknowledged. "Let me have another little piece of that."

"What have you guys been doing since you been here?" Toby asked.

"Martin and I arrived a few days ago, checked out some of the night spots but mostly spent time in our room," Gina answered and sipped water from her glass.

"Trish and I have done some water sports, eaten some fabulous food and we did a few clubs. We've only been here a couple of days. It's been fun," Jim answered, sticking a fork of stir fried vegetables into his mouth before following it up with a piece of steak. "Where are you guys from?"

"Atlanta," Toby said, touching his chest. "Augusta." He pointed an index finger toward Jordan.

"Jordan, do you think you'll ever give up teaching for designing?" Trish asked.

Jordan replied, "I do love teaching, having some input on what's going into these kids' heads is very important to me, but making beautiful clothing is deep in my heart. Teaching allowed me to be able to take care of my family. That being said, if the stars were perfectly aligned for me, I'd be a fashion designer."

"You mentioned earlier that you took care of sibling twins. That was an enormous challenge not to mention sacrifice," Gina said.

Toby was thinking they didn't know the half about Jordan's sacrifices. The young woman was awesome and many times since he met her did he wish he could make her life easier. She deserved something good to happen to her for a change. Her whole life shouldn't be a struggle.

"Have you ever considered relocating? Atlanta, New York or even Miami? Those places are wide open to pursue a fashion career. And, Atlanta wouldn't be far for you," Trish said.

Toby looked at Jordan and they exchanged a smile.

Gina noticed and grinned. "It's hard to believe that you two just met today."

"I rescued her from some guy who was drooling all over himself about her. I had to get her away from that." Toby grinned, looking over at Jordan who was about to give him another jab in the ribs.

"I think my man is quite taken with her," Jim observed and looked at Toby for confirmation.

"That's what I've been saying all day." Trish smiled and after sipping from her tea glass, she looked at Jordan and said, "You would have to do something about that name."

"What's wrong with my name?" Jordan asked, biting off a piece of bread.

"We already have a Jordan and a Banks," Trish said and they all chuckled.

"Well, my middle name is Dakota," Jordan informed and they chuckled some more.

"That's it." Trish snapped her fingers. "Dakota. Now that's a fun name."

"Gee, thanks. I think." Jordan chuckled.

"I love it," Gina said. "Jordan Dakota Banks. Girl, you got the kind of name that belongs in lights."

"Just by adding my middle name, huh?"

Trish lifted her shoulders. "It has a certain ring to it."

The women chuckled.

Trish pushed her plate away and asked, "Which fashion institute did you attend?"

"I didn't go to fashion school," Jordan replied. "It's just something I picked up when I was a kid. I would make my mom so angry because I would use my school paper to sketch and I was always running out of paper."

They chuckled.

"You have that natural ability."

"You just think of an outfit, make a pattern and sew it?" Gina asked.

"I don't use patterns."

"What?" Trish said. "I think that is amazing."

Trish pushed back in her seat and said, "I am stuffed."

"So am I," Jordan said.

"Jordan, you have the most amazing eyes," Gina complimented.

"Thanks."

Then an idea hit Trish and she said to her husband, "Jim, remember that couple we represented a couple of years ago who moved their design house from Philadelphia to Atlanta?"

"Michael and TaNisha Turner," Jim responded.

"Yeah. Why don't we introduce Jordan to them?" Trish said.

"Good idea. That could be a perfect fit," Jim said.

"What are you two talking about?" Jordan inquired.

"There's a couple who is in the fashion business that we represented a few years back and they have a fashion business in Atlanta. We'd be happy to put you in touch with them. They may have some pointers that might be useful," Trish said.

"Would you do that?"

"Sure," Trish assured Jordan, going through her purse for a pen and note pad that she jotted a number on and handed it to Jordan.

Jordan was excited as she accepted the slip of paper. "Thank you so much. You two make my ambitions seem possible."

Jim lifted his glass. "To Jordan," he said.

The others followed, lifting their glasses in a toast.

Toby looked at Jordan and winked. She gave him a smile.

After a moment, Trish said, "Let's get out of here. I hear they've got some terrific shops on the island and I want to do a little shopping."

"I've never heard those two words, 'little' and 'shopping' together coming out of my wife's mouth," Jim said and the couples roared.

"Trish said, "I want another bathing suit."

Jim said, "Sure you do. You need another bathing suit like you need another hole in your head."

"I only want one," Trish said but the look on her face told a different story.

"That's what you say now," he replied. Trish could have anything her heart desired. Everyone could see that Jim and Trish were very much in love and her wish was his command.

Before leaving the restaurant and a generous tip to the waitress' delight, they inquired and were told the largest mall on the island was only four blocks away as well as a number of fashionable shops along the way. As they walked towards the mall taking in the sights, Toby couldn't take his eyes off of Jordan and it's been that way from the time they met on the beach that morning.

When they came upon a group of kids playing instruments and doing their native dance along the sidewalk,

the couples joined in and danced with
the kids under the bright sun shining
from a vivid blue sky.

CHAPTER 5

At the mall, as the women went off
to shop, the men found an area where
they could sit, have a smoke and

engage in small talk from stocks, politics, and the economy to health care and cars.

As the women went through the clothing racks, Trish approached Jordan with an item in her hands and said, "You know Toby is in love with you, don't you?"

Jordan's eye popped wide open in surprise.

"You noticed that too?" Gina said, holding several items in her hand she was going to check out. "I saw that. That boy's got it bad for you, girl."

"What are you two talking about?" Jordan asked, frown on her face.

"You know exactly what we're talking about," Gina said, giving her a devious look.

"A blind man could see how that man feels about you, girlfriend," Trish said.

"You girls have been watching too many of those Lifetime movies."
They chuckled.

"I love a good Lifetime movie, but I also know that boy has got it bad for you."

"That man doesn't even know me," Jordan said. "Toby and I are just getting to know each other and that won't be much longer because I leave for home tomorrow, so there."

"I'll say it one more time and then I'm done with it," Trish said. "That man is in love with you and that's a fact."

"I'm sure you're wrong but just so you know, I'm one week out of a relationship that didn't end well. It left me with a broken heart, so I'm not trying to get involved with anyone else no time soon."

"You don't look nor act like a woman who is heartbroken," Gina said.

"I guess I'm adapting to my situation," Jordan said, then added, "Actually, I have Toby to thank for my current disposition because he pulled me out of the pool of misery I was drowning in."

"He obviously cares a great deal for you. I see you trying to avoid eye contact with him sometimes so I know you're sensing something but you may as well get over it and go with the flow. Heck, you got a fine young man who wants to lead you away from a broken heart situation and protect you and you are afraid to take a chance.

Girl, you had better grab that man by the balls, hold on tight and let him take you from misery to paradise. That's what I would do. I wouldn't let the brotha out of my sight," Gina said.

"Uh hmmmm," Trish concurred.

After a while, the ladies had finished shopping and they went to claim their men. Gina and Trish were loaded down with purchases while Jordan carried two small shopping bags.

"Did you get something nice for yourself?" Toby asked, taking the bags from Jordan's hand to carry along with the bag he was carrying.

"No, she didn't," Gina answered. "She bought gifts for her siblings and a neighbor."

Toby smiled.

"Hey guys, since this is Jordan's last night on the island, why don't we take her out and show her a good time," Trish suggested, handing Jim her bags.

"Swim suits?" Jim whispered, raising his eyebrows, a crooked smile on his face.

"Among other things." Trish smiled back and turned away, wiggling her hips playfully at him.

"Going to a club tonight is a great idea," Gina agreed, handing her bags to Martin.

"You guys don't have to do that," Jordan said, looking from one person to the next. When she made eye contact with Toby, his smile, his lips, his teeth were electrifying. Her earlier conversation rushed back to her and she quickly turned away from his gaze, feeling affected by it, still not sure what it meant nor did she want to know.

"Of course we're going to turn up with you tonight," Gina said, winking at Martin.

When they left the mall, they saw that it was raining again.

Gina glanced up at the sky. "Oh, hell to the naaw. It's raining again. I need an umbrella."

"Aaah, it's just a little rain," Trish said.

"I told you I don't have that wet and wear hair. What I have up here," Gina pouted, placing a hand on her head, "requires a hot iron when this gets wet."

"Your hair is fine," Jordan said, touching Gina's long auburn hair.

"Give it time," Gina said, going through her purse. Locating a hair clip, she pulled her hair up and put in the clip to hold it in place.

Before long, the rain had stopped. They took a taxi back to their hotels. The taxi stopped at Jordan's hotel first. Gina looked at her watch. "It's six fifteen. Why don't we pick you up in an hour? We can have dinner, then hit a couple of hot clubs and get turnt."

"Okay. I'll see you guys then." Jordan got out of the taxi and with Toby climbing out after her. She waved to her new friends and Toby walked her to her hotel door.

Toby smiled at Jordan and ran his hands down her arms. "I'll see you later."

"Okay." She smiled back.

Toby turned and practically skipped back to the waiting taxi.

Jordan entered the hotel lobby and took the elevator up to her room. In her room, she removed the damp clothes that she hung over the back of a chair to dry. She pulled a robe from her suitcase, slipped into it, and then she pulled from the suitcase a pair of black stilettos and a tiny black dress that she laid on the bed. She didn't have much time to get dressed for her last night in Montego Bay, but earlier she'd seen a dress in one of the boutiques. She couldn't afford the dress but she could make it when she returned home. She pulled her sketch pad and pencil from the dresser, sat on the bed and took a few minutes to put a quick sketch on paper. Now, she could think about what the evening would entail and the thought of seeing Toby again before returning to America made her smile.

Jordan turned on the water in the shower and simultaneously, her doorbell rang. She tied the sash to her robe, walked to the door and when she opened it, she was surprised to see one of the hotel employees standing there with a gift bag in her hand.

"Miss Jordan Dakota Banks," said the young woman with the rich island accent.

"Yes."

"This is for you, ma'am."

"For me?" Jordan asked in surprise. What? Who?"

The young woman handed the package to Jordan, she accepted it.

The young woman turned to leave and Jordan said, "Wait just a moment, please."

Knowing Jordan's intentions, the young woman smiled and said, "Thank you, ma'am, but the sender has already taken care of everything."

Jordan pulled a few bills from her purse anyway. "Please take this. I'd like you to have it."

The young woman accepted the tip and bowing her head to Jordan, said, "Thank you."

Jordan carried the bag over to her bed; she removed the card and read. 'Please wear this for me tonight. Toby.'

Jordan reached into the bag. She lifted from it a gorgeous white rayon and silk dress, the same dress that she'd admired earlier in the boutique and had sketched its likeness moments ago.

Jordan held the dress up and looked at it. She couldn't believe that Toby had been so observant. And although she appreciated his kindness, his generous gesture, she knew she couldn't accept something so expensive from someone she barely knew, yet she didn't want to disappoint him either. He was so nice. She would find a way to let him know he should return the dress tomorrow.

In the next minute, the phone in her room rang. She answered it.

"Did you receive the gift?" Toby asked.
Jordan's heart skipped a beat. "Yes. Yes, I did."

"If I have learned anything about you, is that you're always giving to someone but you have a difficult time accepting things from others. I'd like you to accept something for a change. Would you please do that for me?"

"I really love the dress. It is amazing…."

"I hear a *but* in there somewhere."

"Toby, it was a lovely gesture and I appreciate it, but I can't accept it."

"I'm asking you, no I'm begging you to please accept the dress as a gift. No strings attached except I'd like to see you in it. Would you please wear it tonight,…for me?"

Jordan didn't know what to say. What could she say? This was a genuine gesture of kindness and she did appreciate it. "This dress is too expensive. It's at least a week's salary for me." She chuckled.

"You deserve it, and I can't wait to see you in it. That fabric is gonna be so happy," he said, chuckling."

"Funny guy."She chuckled along with him.

"So, will you wear the dress?"

"Yes! I will wear the dress."

"Then, I'll see you shortly."

Jordan quickly showered, rubbed a lightly fragranced lotion on her body and applied a little makeup. She combed her hair so that it hung over one shoulder. She added pearl earrings, a bracelet and she slipped her feet into a pair of metallic strapped shoes. She slipped on the dress with a low neckline that showed off a lot of cleavage and a single button that clutched at the waist, outlining her hourglass figure. She checked herself in the full length mirror she was satisfied with how she looked.

Jordan checked the digital clock on the bedside table. Eight fifteen. She grabbed her purse and left her room. When she arrived downstairs, the others were waiting for her. If she had a second of doubt about how she looked in that dress, the look on Toby's face when he saw her told her everything.

He walked up to greet her. In a quick glance, his look took in everything from her well defined legs, her tiny waist to her voluptuous breasts. "You are a knockout," he said and he meant it. Toby had never seen anyone as beautiful as Jordan and he wanted her to know how he felt.

"Amen to that," Jim said.

Toby devoured Jordan with his eyes.

Gina linked her arm with Jordan and whispered, "Girl, you look sensational and that man can't take his eyes off of you."

"Oh, hush up," Jordan teased.

They left the hotel. It was a warm night, the sky had darkened; a deep blue rose in the east while westward, crimson reds and yellows trailed the sun as it sank. They walked out on the street. When Toby put his hand on Jordan's hand, the air filled with electricity. Before she could ease her hand out of his, there was a burst of fireworks that caused the three women to scream simultaneously as Jordan threw herself into Toby's arms.

"It's alright," Toby said, gently squeezing her. "You are safe with me."

When the fireworks stopped, Jordan extracted herself from Toby's arms and they went to the restaurant where they chitchat while dining on the island's finest cuisine.

Later, on the way to a popular nightclub, Jordan caught a glimpse of the side of Toby's face when he finally wasn't looking at her. The man was outrageously handsome, dressed in a dark suit and white shirt opened at the neck. It took her a long moment to draw her eyes away.

When they arrived at Jamaican Nights, the dimly lit club was crowded, the music was popping, and the crowd was energetic. It appeared all eyes were on Jordan. Toby took her hand in his as they were led to the table.

Toby had called earlier to make reservations and they were seated at a large table near the center of the room. A cocktail waitress took their drink orders. Trish suggested champagne.

"Champagne, it is," Toby said, turning his eyes away from Jordan for a moment. When he turned back to her, he whispered, "Did I tell you that you look amazing."

Smiling demurely, she responded, "Yes, and you look great also." It was true. Jordan had never met anyone as handsome or as sexy as Toby. The man was super fine and he didn't appear to be aware of just how fine he really was.

When the champagne arrived and each glass was filled, Gina said, "I'd like to propose a toast." They all lifted their glasses. "To Jordan. May you take your destiny into your own hands and embark on the career of your choice, your passion and just be happy. Do your thing, girl."

"Here, here," Trish said, and they clicked their glasses.

The club's deejay played a combination of island music and popular American tunes. When an up tempo crowd favorite began to play, Trish was the first to push her chair back and jumped up. "Come on, Jim. Let's get this party started," she said.

Jim got out of his seat and caught his wife's hand. "Lead the way, baby," he said, following her to the dance floor.

Martin and Gina was the next couple to hit the dance floor.

Jordan was looking at the dancers on the floor. When she turned to look at Toby, she was surprised to see him staring at her. The look in his eyes made her breathless, just as it had done when they first met that morning on the beach.

When she could breathe again, she asked, "Is something wrong?"

"Not at all," he replied, thinking all he wanted to do was get her to want him half as much as he wanted her. Then, he smiled. "Dance with me."

"Okay."

Toby led Jordan to the dance floor. Gina and Trish both gave Jordan a thumb up.

After they had been dancing a short time, Jordan leaned in and said, "You're a really good dancer."

"So are you."

After a while a ballad played, giving Toby the perfect opportunity to wrap Jordan in his arms and hold her, and hold her, and hold her. He gently drew her to him, he wrapped his arms around her waist and holding her close, he closed his eyes and as he enjoyed the fragrance she was wearing, he savored the feel of her body pressed closely to his. As they moved sensuously to the music, Toby couldn't believe he was actually holding this beautiful creature in his arms and feeling all the things he was feeling. If he had one wish, it would be that moment would last forever.

The night wore on. They danced to one beautiful ballad after the other, and she'd been acutely aware of how their closeness, their movements were affecting him. He was so immensely male. Sometime later, the club lights came up, announcing closing time. Jordan looked around the club and saw that Trish and Jim were also dancing but Gina and Martin had been sitting at the table, staring into each other's eyes over a glass of wine.

When the music stopped, Toby whispered against Jordan's ear, "I don't want to let you go."

She pulled away to look into his eyes. "No?"

"Hell no!" he said and he meant it. He wanted to hold her in his arms all night, forever if he could.

"I've had an incredible time."

"It doesn't have to end here."

"I know but it's really late and I have got a plane to catch in the afternoon."

"Spend the week with me."

"Excuse me," Jordan said, taken aback by that statement.

"I meant stay here on the island another week. Keep your own room. I'll keep mine, we can meet for breakfast and just allow the day to unfold. We could spend time just getting to know each other. I would love that. I feel I'm beginning to know the woman you are and I am damn happy with what I do know. We could explore the island together, see how the natives live. I'd be more than happy to take care of your accommodations. It would be great. What do you say? "

"I appreciate your generosity but I couldn't ask you to do that."

"You're not asking. I'm offering." Toby waited a moment. When all he got was a weak smile, he said, "You deserve to give yourself this time."

"Honestly, I wish I could but…."

Toby interrupted her. "We're talking about only one week." He lifted one finger to her. "One week. What's stopping you from giving yourself that little bit of love?"

"I've been here a week and I've got to admit it didn't start off so well but after meeting you today, this has been the best time I've had all week. Today has been a day in paradise and I have you to thank for this, but it's time to get back to reality."

"There's nothing I can do to get you to change your mind?"

"As much as I'd like to, I've got to decline your wonderful offer."

Jordan and Tobin joined the others back at the table.

"So are you love birds ready to blow this joint?" Gina asked, looking from Jordan to Toby.

"I suppose we'd better. It looks as though we're closing down the place as it is," Toby said and they all laughed.

As they got up to leave, Gina walked up closely to Jordan and whispered to her, "You can say what you want but that man right there," she pointed a finger in Toby's direction, "He's gonna be your baby daddy."

They left the restaurant with Jordan and Gina giggling out loud.

On the ride back to the hotel, Gina was sitting in Martin's lap and they were making out like teenagers.

"Hey you guys, get a room," Jim said and laughter filled the taxi.

"Why don't we all go to my suite and have a nightcap?" Toby suggested.

"You sure you don't want to spend some alone time with Jordan?" Jim asked.

"Well, I'm hoping she'll join us," Toby said.

"I should call it a night and get ready for my trip later this afternoon," Jordan said.

"Oh, come on. Don't be a party pooper," Gina said, pulling away from Martin.

"Be quiet and kiss me woman," Martin said and begun kissing Gina again.

Trish said, with a wave of her hand, "Forget those two."

They all chuckled.

"Come on, Jordan. We'll make sure that you get to the airport on time to catch your plane," Jim assured her.

"Come on, Jordan," Trish insisted.

Jordan and Tobin looked at each other, shaking her head she said, "Okay, I'll go spend a little more time with you guys."

"Great," Trish cheered Jordan's decision.

Jim glanced over at Martin and Gina. "Do those two ever come up for air?"

Gina and Martin stopped kissing. She looked around and asked, "Are we there yet?"

"Yes, Gina, we're here," Trish informed. "How long have you two been married again? You guys are behaving like sex starved teens." She chuckled.

They got out of the taxi and entered the hotel that had a huge expansive lobby, several lounging areas and a bar that extended an entire wall. The hotel lobby was magnificent in its décor from the beautiful furnishing, the oriental rugs, expensive oil paintings adorning the walls and huge tropical plants throughout. They took the elevator to the fourteenth floor; Toby led them to a beautiful suite where they were greeted by white sheer curtains billowing from the breezes, coming from the ocean below.

"Come in everyone and find a seat," he offered. "I've got a couple of bottles of wine in the frig," Toby said, putting on the music. "Be right back," he said, heading toward the small kitchenette.

"I'll help," Jordan said, dropping her purse on the coffee table and followed him.

Toby turned to face her. "I'm glad you decided to come."

"So am I," she replied. She couldn't deny she was enjoying her time with the group, especially her time with Toby. Being with him had taken her mind off of her own problems and her pain.

Toby slipped his arms around Jordan's waist, drew her close to him and his lips came dangerously close to hers.

Looking into his eyes, she could easily get caught up in the moment, but she managed to slip out of his grasp and asked, "Where did you say those glasses are?"

Toby ran a hand across his face and said, "They're right over here." He went over and removed glasses from the cabinet above the sink. After pulling two bottles of wine from the refrigerator that Jordan took from his hands, placed them with the glasses on a tray, they went back to join the others and where they found Gina sitting in Martin's lap on one end of the couch, kissing passionately.

Jim got up from his chair, pulled Trish into his arms and they began to dance.

When Gina and Martin came up for air, Jordan asked, "How long have you two been married?"
Gina quickly answered, "Five years, but who's counting."

"I know that's right," Trish said and reached over and gave Gina a high five.

Toby filled the wine glasses and Jordan passed them out.

When everyone had a glass in their hand, Toby said, "I'd like to make a toast. To new friends, I hope you will continue to be as happy and in love as you are at this moment."

After the toast, more than an hour later, they chitchatted and laughed and danced, but the majority of the time, Gina and Martin spent their time locked in each other's embrace, kissing. Finally, Jim got up. "Hey guys, this has been great but we're outta here."

Gina leaped to her feet, pulling Martin with her. After saying their goodbyes with a promise to keep in touch, Gina winked at Jordan before leaving her and Toby alone.

Toby closed the door and walked with her back over to the couch. "Finish your wine and I'll see you back at your hotel," he said.

Jordan had spent an entire day with Toby and she knew he was a nice man and felt by now that he could be trusted so she agreed to stay with him a while. "Okay."

"So, did you have fun today? I hope it was as much fun for you as it was for me. It has been one incredible day for me, seeing you enjoying yourself meant everything."

"It was the best day that I've had in a long time."

"Oh yeah?"

"Yeah." When they met, Toby had told her everything about his family, when his father died, the relationship between he and his mother. "I never knew my father or the twins' father. There wasn't a father figure in my home. I can't ever remember a man living in our home and taking care of us when my mother was alive."

Jordan shifted in her place on the couch. She remembered there was always a stream of men coming and going at their house. She'd hear them coming in late at night and leaving early in the morning before she and the twins got up. She had no idea which of her mother's numerous sexual partners had deposited the seeds that created her and her siblings. As Jordan got older, she realized it was either a miracle or a blessing that there weren't more children in their family and for that she couldn't have been more grateful.

Her mother was a party girl, went out and most nights, leaving Jordan to look after her sister and brother, she brought someone home with her. Jordan always knew because she could hear their voices and movement coming from her mother's room. They never knew who was there. They slept in one room. The only time they got to sleep with their mother was when she didn't have some leech in her bed, crawling all over her or when there was a storm. The twins were afraid of the lightning and especially the thunder. Their mother would allow them to come into her room, they'd climbed into her bed and she'd wrap her arms around them and protect them from whatever was going on outside. Their mother always impressed upon them to do as she said, not what she did.

"Mama was strict on us, especially Steffie and I. She always said that a young lady should behave a certain way. She made sure that we went to school and did well, always stressing the importance of getting a good education. So in her mixed up life, she loved her children and we all knew it. When she died, I was so angry at her. I hated her for leaving me. I thought I would never get over the anger, the hate I felt for her. It took a long time but I did get over it and eventually I forgave her."

Jordan changed the subject. "You must be bored out of your mind. I have been running my mouth all day."

"You could never bore me. You're a pleasure to be with, wonderful to talk with and amazing to look at."

"This has been one of the most wonderful days that I have ever had."
"Jim and Trish and Gina and Martin? They were fun, weren't they?"
"They were great. I liked them a lot and the unusual way that we met was something in itself. Who would ever believe that?" Jordan and Toby chuckled.

"Did the girls let you in on the secret?"

"What secret? No one told me anything about any secret?"

"Gina and Martin?"

"What about Gina and Martin?"

"They aren't married."

"What are you talking about?" Jordan wanted to know, a furrow in her brow.

"No, they are not married to each other. Gina is single but Martin is married to someone else. Gina used to be his office assistant, they started fooling around, fell in love, and they've been seeing each other the past five years."

"They're lovers. It makes sense. I see why they had been going at it almost non-stop. They had to get it in before returning back to their individual lives."

"I guess."

"Why do you think they weren't truthful about their relationship? They're consenting adults and we don't know them from Adam. I don't understand the lies."

"Who knows? Maybe they just get off on this secretive thing. I don't know why people do the things they do."

Jordan shrugged. "To each his own."

Then it became quiet for a moment as they stared out the open window that had a full view of the ocean. The sounds of the ocean, the fragrance from the flowers coming through the open windows were soothing.

"I got my heart broken once. It was many years ago." Toby began, breaking the silence. Jordan turned in her seat to look at him. He looked at her. "Virginia Mayfield. Jenny. She was an only child, spoiled, popular, intelligent, not to mention gorgeous, and I didn't think I could live without her. Wanted to spend the rest of my life with her"

For a second, Jordan thought she felt a small pang of jealousy, but she quickly dismissed it. Why would she be jealous of any relationships Toby might have had or is involved with now? She asked, "Was it love at first sight for both of you?"

"Yeah, I think so," he replied and fell silent again.

"What happened?"

The stern angles of his face seemed to turn almost bashful. "The first two years were great. She meant everything to me and I'd never been happier." He rested his head back against the back of the couch. "I was in medical school and a lot of my time was devoted to helping to look after my mother. Jenny didn't think I was spending enough time with her and perhaps she was right. Then, I found out she was cheating on me." His jaw tightened.

"I'm sorry."

Toby continued as though she hadn't spoken. "It broke my heart and even though I promised that I'd spend more time with her and get our relationship back on track, she was done with us and what we had. Jenny was done with me. She was ready to move on. So, it was over, she went her way, I went mine and since that time, I've not been seriously involved with anyone."

"You haven't given up on women, have you?"

"No way! I date often but no serious commitments."

"Are you open to love or are you content with things the way they are?"

"For years I'd been perfectly happy with the way things were, but to my surprise, I've had a change of heart."

Jordan raised her eyebrows. "You care to elaborate?"

He combed his fingers through her hair. "What do you intend to do when you return to Georgia?"

"I don't know," she tugged at her earlobe, "but I definitely don't want you worrying about me. I'll manage."

"Do you always do that?"

"What?"

"Tug at your earlobe. You do it a lot."

"I didn't realize that."

After a moment, Toby said, "You know you really don't have to go through this alone. I would do anything for you, Jordan," Toby said and he knew with every fiber of his being that if he had the chance to be there for this woman, he would and he knew it would make all the difference in her life—and his. "You don't have to just manage. You're much too special for that. You deserve so much better than that."

Jordan knew what he was getting at and thought for a moment before saying, "Toby, I'm just getting out of a relationship that ended badly;

therefore, I don't intend to get involved in another relationship for a long time," she said looking off into the distance before adding, "if ever."

"I would never hurt you, Jordan," Toby said and he meant it. When she looked at him, she could see that truth in his eyes. "I don't want you to go back home and sit on the sideline and be afraid to take a great big juicy bite out of life. Sometimes things happen that change us forever, sometime they make our lives better, other times, not so much, but you don't strike me as a woman who sits and watches as the world passes by. I'm not always right but I'm seldom wrong. I'm willing to bet that you're the kind of woman who charts her own course, knows what she wants and when she is knocked down, she picks herself up and moves on without as much as a backward glance."

She turned to look at him. "Is that how you really see me?"

"Absolutely. First of all, you're the most gorgeous woman that I've ever had the pleasure of laying my eyes on. You are intelligent, sophisticated, classy, a woman with her head on her shoulders—a woman in charge."

She felt his fingers tips massaging the back of her neck. She smiled. "I really should be getting back to the hotel."

He was silent for a moment before asking, "What time is your flight?"

"Two o'clock."

"And, I can't convince you to stay another week?"

"I'm afraid not."

"Promise me one thing. If you ever want to talk, call me. Anytime, day or night."

"You may be sorry you extended that offer, if I start calling you at three o'clock in the morning."

"Not a chance," Toby said and he was certain of that but wasn't at all certain why he made the next statement. "If you let me, I would love you so damn hard and so damn good that you would never walk away from me or let me walk away from you."

Really?"

"It would be so easy because if you were my woman, I wouldn't be going nowhere."

Is he talking about sex, lust, love? She wondered, or has he completely lost his mind?

"I…I don't know what to say," she stuttered.

Toby gazed into Jordan's eyes and said honestly, "I care about you and just as I know my own name, I know I always will. You're already in my mind, my heart and I'd like to keep you there! Always!"

"You know you're confusing me right now."

"I don't want to do that. Let me put everything on the table. Do you believe in love at first sight?"

"Yeah, I believe it happens."

"It's never happened to you?"

"No!"

"It's happened to me twice, but it's different this time." Jordan didn't comment. She just listened. "Somewhere between this morning and right now," he used his hands to emphasize his thoughts, "I fell in love with you."

Jordan was incredulous. She threw back her head and laughed, but when she looked at him again, she saw a serious expression on his handsome face. In the next moment, the laughter was gone and surprise registered on her face. Quickly recovering, she said, "Toby, that's ridiculous." When she saw that his expression hadn't changed, she said, "You can't mean that."

"But I can, and I do."

"Are you seriously telling me you're in love with me or are you plying me with alcohol and telling me you're in love with me with the idea that you'll score later?"

"I've never gotten a woman drunk to screw her! Never had to!"

The last thing Jordan wanted to do was hurt Toby's feelings. He'd been nothing but kind to her and had behaved like the perfect gentleman from the time they met. "I'm sorry if I insulted you. That wasn't my intention."

"You didn't. I'm telling you that I fell in love with you today and that is true. It's as simple as that." As she stared back at him, something deep inside her, something at her core, wanted to believe what he was saying. Still it was difficult to convince herself. Both, her intuition and her emotions told her to tread lightly—not get taken in and allow her feelings to become involved. "So there, I said it.

What do you think about that?" He asked.

There was something else going on inside her. It was hard to explain yet impossible to ignore.

"Do you think you could ever love me?"

Jordan looked at him. "Why are we having this conversation, Toby? You can't possibly be serious."

"I couldn't be more serious."

Shaking her head, she said, "Toby, all I want or need is a peaceful, quiet place in my life. That's all I can handle right now." After a moment's pause, she said, "I'm sure the day will come when that'll all change and I will want someone in my life. Someone who is going in the same direction as I am."

"Do you think you could ever love me?" He repeated.

"Don't do this. Please. You and I are practically strangers and right now, love is the last thing we should be talking about."

"What are we waiting for? What's to stop us from loving each other? It's not like we are kids and need permission."

Jordan closed her eyes and for an instant, the wine she drank swam with her thoughts. Would she let herself dare to dream of the possibilities that something like this could open up between Toby and her. What difference would it make if they enjoyed each other while on the island and it didn't go further? Who would it hurt? After a moment, she thought she had to put thoughts like those out of her mind. Regardless to how vulnerable she was feeling, she did realize that that kind of thinking was ridiculous.

"There's something I tell my patients all the time," Toby began, "live your best life today because we don't know what tomorrow will bring. For what it's worth, Jordan, I do love you."

"It is sweet of you to say that and I appreciate it but all I can handle right now is friendship."

"Of course, we will be friends. Isn't that the basis for most good relationships?"

"I believe so." Seeing the look in Toby's eyes, she added, "I don't want to get hurt again, Toby. Can you understand that?"

"Of course I can, but you can be sure that I would never hurt you. I care just too damn much." Toby was looking deeply into Jordan's eyes when a beautiful ballad began to play from his CD collection. He pulling her to him, he said, "Dance with me."

Their bodies came together and standing body to body, she found herself relaxing under his hands and his watchful eyes. He pulled her closer, loving the way she fit in his arms. As they danced, she could feel his heart beating against her chest.

He pushed his head back to look at her and looking down into her eyes, smiling, he said, "Hey you."

"Hey you," she replied, returning his smile.

"I want you and I think it's fair to let you know that I don't give up easily. I've wanted you from the moment I saw you."

Jordan stiffened for a moment and in silence, they studied each other. He reached up to touch her cheek. His hand lingered there while his eyes traveled her face, from her beautiful eyes, the curve of her cheekbones to her luscious lips. Unable to resist the temptation to cover her mouth with his, he lowered his head toward her. Jordan's lips parted to protest, but his lips descended upon hers, causing her words to become trapped and were spoken directly into his mouth. He kissed her, rolling his tongue over her lips before probing his tongue deeply into her mouth. No one had ever kissed Jordan that way. No one had ever made her feel the way Toby had and with a single kiss. He pulled back a moment, then pausing only briefly before his mouth was devouring hers again. His hands splayed on her back as he drew her even closer to him, flattening her chest against his.

Toby pulled back again, unable to believe he was actually holding this lovely creature and kissing her. He gently kissed the corner of her mouth, he ran his tongue along her lips again before thrusting his tongue deeply into her mouth. Jordan moaned softly as she sank deeper into his embrace, the kiss. It was sweet, so unbelievably sweet that neither wanted to stop—couldn't bear to stop. As the kiss continued, a shiver feathered across Jordan's skin from head to toe, and she knew at that instant, she wanted the kiss to go on forever. After a moment, she pulled away from him.

What happened next surprised Jordan more than Toby. She returned her mouth to his, seeking out his lips, his tongue. She clutched frantically at his shoulders, his back, then her arms went up around his neck and she pushed her tongue inside his mouth and allowed it to play. Their tongues dueled and the kiss grew deeper, seeking, demanding. They settled into a kiss that was so sensual, so needy, so telling. They couldn't get enough of each other as they both swayed from side to side, almost losing their balance.

Toby's hand rose up to cup one of Jordan's breasts. His thumb caressed her nipple. Before Jordan realized what was happening, Toby had slid his hand under the fabric of her dress, lifted her breast to his lips and began sucking hungrily on it. Jordan nearly screamed his name as she shivered from undulating pleasure. When Toby tore his mouth from her breast, his breath came in raw, panting gasps, and as his huge erect member moved sensuously and ferociously against her, she wasn't able to remember why she'd come to Montego Bay or how she happened to be in the arms of this handsome stranger. She did know that she was enjoying the feelings that were flowing through her and the ache between her legs was so intense that it causing her to desperately want to lie down somewhere—anywhere, spread her legs wide apart and welcomed him inside her inner world. He tore his mouth from hers and in a breathless moment, he ran a hand alongside her face and said, "I love you, Jordan Banks. I love you so much."

She lifted her head, opened her eyes and looked up at him. Her eyes were huge, dilated. She trembled at the way he was looking down at her, the intensity of need evident in his eyes. As they stood gazing into each other's eyes, she wondered whether she could ever put those kisses out of her heart, her mind like they had never happened.

Only a short time passed before Toby was devouring Jordan's mouth again in a long, lingering kiss that was filled with all the magic it could possess. When he pulled away, breaking the kiss, her eyes remained closed in anticipation of the next one. His mouth covered hers and he begun to suck her lips ferociously. He reached down, cupped her buttocks in his hands and moved her hard against his hard, thick, long member.

After a series of moans and groans and thrusting their bodies fiercely against each other, this time, it was Jordan who broke the kiss. She said, "Toby, I'm sorry. I didn't mean for this to happen."

He took a deep breath. "Don't blame yourself, baby. You didn't do anything wrong. How is it wrong to respond to your feelings? I wanted that as much as you. Probably more. What am I saying? I am certain I want you more."

She extracted herself from him, went over to the table and picked up her purse. "I'd better go."

Toby ran his hand down across his face. He went over to her and caught her arms. "You don't have to go." He lifted one hand and rubbed his thumb over her lips that were swollen from his kisses. "I want you. I can't deny that. I want you so much that I ache," he said ruefully, "but I would never do anything that you didn't want to do. You've been through too many emotional upheavals and I would never add to that. I care too much. When the time is right, we will *both* know it." He dropped a light kiss on her lips. "Besides, it builds character in a man when he doesn't always get what he wants." He laughed a little.

Unable to meet his bold penetrating stare, she quickly turned her head away from him. "This is so unfair to you."

"Why don't you stay and let me take care of you tonight?" He took her hand in his. "I promise I'll behave."

She looked up at him. "Toby, you have no idea who I am."

"Perhaps not but what I do know, I'm liking….a hell of a lot." He sighed deeply. "Look, I know what you've been through and I understand where you're coming from but I'd like to pursue what I am feeling with you. I know you need time to get where I know that I am and just know, I'll wait for you. If there is some reason for me to wait."

"Do you know how perfectly insane that all sounds?"

"It sounds perfectly logical to me."

"I really don't believe you."

"You don't believe me or do you have questions about what I am saying?"

"I don't know. It all just seems so ridiculous."

"Because I find you to be so wonderful, you're so damn fine and I want to know so much more about you. I would really love to see where we can take this."

"There's more," she said slowly.

"What, then?"

Jordan shook her head to clear the thoughts that were floating around, making her dizzy. "Everything; you, me, this whole business about *us*. We're from vastly different worlds." She shook her head again. "Let's just not talk about it anymore." She had to get away from that conversation, from him before her desire ran completely out of control. She knew her defenses could start crashing down any second. "Can we just forget what just happened?"

"All we did was kiss."

"It was so much more than that," she said thinking about how their bodies connected and responded to each other. How he'd wedged himself between her legs and ground hard and sensuously against her and how she had responded.

"If that's what you want." He said, pulling her from her reverie.

"I think that's best."

Resisting the urge to challenge her, Toby said simply, "Okay."

Jordan turned to walk away. Toby caught her hand and gently pulled her back into his arms. "Let me make a suggestion." He wrapped his arms around her waist.

She pressed her face against his chest. "Go ahead."

"Why not spend what's left of the night here and I'll take you to your hotel later. You sleep in the bed. I'll hang out here on the couch."

"If I do stay here with you, I'll sleep on the couch, and that is not negotiable."

Toby lifted his arms in surrender. "Alright. I'll get some pillows and a blanket." He kissed her once more, left the room and returned moments later with the pillow and blanket.

After they said goodnight, Toby left the room. Jordan sat on the couch and wondered whether she was making a mistake; first by spending the night in Toby's suite and secondly, feeling the way she did about this virtual stranger. She didn't know as she inhaled deeply, remembering the scent of his cologne playing in her mind, what she did know was how much she was going to miss when she returned home.

CHAPTER 6

Jordan awoke later that morning on the couch in Toby's hotel room and suddenly, she realized that someone was holding her hand. She opened her eyes and saw Toby. His face lit up. He was sitting on the floor, holding her hand and smiling at her, his mouth widening into one of the most devastating smiles that she'd ever seen.

"Good morning." His smile was bright and open, and his eyes fringed with thick dark lashes that took her breath away.

"Good morning," Jordan replied, staring unblinkingly into his eyes. "How long have you been sitting there watching me sleep?"

"I came back out when I saw that you were asleep," he said and at that moment, he knew that in the light of day that the alcohol he drank last night had nothing to do with him telling Jordan he was in love with her. He was in love with this girl. He was in love with her last night. He was in love her this morning. And, he knew he always would love her. He'd never known anyone like her. She was the most unselfish, considerate person, to say nothing of being genuinely nice and so totally unaware of her physical beauty.

Jordan was fully clothed except her shoes had been removed. She sat up on the couch. "I can't believe I slept in this beautiful dress."

"It's just a dress."

"It's a very nice dress—a dress that you gave me." She ran her hands down the fabric. "No one has ever done anything like this for me before."

"Then things like this should happen more often. You certainly deserve it."

Jordan tried to get up.

"There is no need to rush. Your plane doesn't leave for a while."

Jordan smiled. Then, she noticed the tie Toby was wearing last night wedged between the cushions of the sofa where she spent the night. She picked up the tie with the Armani label, folded it and placed it on the coffee table.

"Well, we didn't exactly spend the night together but then again, we did, but your virtue is still intact."

"This is not something that I do," Jordan said. "I've never been involved in a one night stand before." After the words left Jordan's mouth, she immediately felt very high school. She was a grown woman and here she was behaving like some innocent child. And, she was far from innocent.

"You think I'm judging you because you stayed in my room last night?"

"I don't know. I just wanted you to know that although I'm not a prude by any means, I don't make it a habit of spending the night alone with a strange man."

"And, I thought we were friends." Toby grinned.

Jordan grinned back at him and shook her head. Then she checked the time. "What about breakfast? Aren't we meeting the others downstairs?"

"Yes!"

"I'm not going to have time to go back to the hotel and change and I certainly can't wear this dress." She looked down at herself.

"I've got something in there that I'm sure will be suitable for you to wear to breakfast."

"Are you kidding me?"

"No, actually I'm not. I've got some pants and a shirt in the closet that I'm sure will serve very well. You know how you ladies can use a man's shirt, roll up the sleeves put on some makeup, comb your hair and the outfit looks like it was something you bought for yourself. And you being a fashion designer, I'm willing to bet you will make it work."

You sound as though you've had some experience at this.

He didn't respond to that. She said, "Get me that shirt, please."

Toby left the room and returned shortly saying, "This is for you." He handed her a pale blue shirt and white Bermuda shorts.

Jordan took the items from his extended hand. "This is what you want me to wear. They are huge." She chuckled and he joined in.

"Those are gonna look great on you."

Jordan showered first and when Toby came out of the bathroom, she was already dressed. He watched her beautiful full lips spread and curve into a pearly white smile while her eyes sparkled and danced in a face that was exquisitely beautiful. As he gazed at her, he wanted to take her into his arms, kiss her some more and never let her go.

His Bermuda shorts fitted her like Capris. She'd fastened only three buttons on the shirt and tied knots in the tail that hung over the pants, transforming the pieces into a casual woman's outfit.

When Toby saw her, he said, "Do you look good in everything?"

Jordan walked toward him and spun around. "Does it look okay?"

"You look fantastic."

"Great. Let's go," she said, picking up her purse, and she and Toby went out the door.

They entered the hotel lobby and saw the other couples waiting. Gina's lips curled in a sly smile when she and Jordan made eye contact. Gina rushed over to Jordan and Toby, linked her arm with Jordan's, leaned in and whispered in her ear, "Where did you get those clothes?"

"We all have our secrets," Jordan whispered back to Gina and they chuckled.

Gina's eyes held a happy glint. "So you spent last night with him."

"Not in the way that you're thinking."

"And, what way is that, Darling?" Gina continued to smile as she looked at Jordan.

"Nothing happened, Gina."

Gina smile faded. "What?"

"Nothing happened."

"You let all of that fine brotha go to waste?"

"I'm afraid so."

"Why?"

"It just wasn't the right time."

"To each her own." With that Gina went back and linked her arm with her Martin as they entered the restaurant where they had breakfast.

Toby drove Jordan to the airport close to departure time. After checking in at the ticket counter, he walked her to the cutoff point where they stood, looking into each other's eyes saying goodbye.

"I should be on that plane with you," Toby declared.
"You could."

"You're gonna be just fine."

"I know. I'll keep busy; take in some cultural events, see a few movies, you know."

"Keeping busy is the thing to do." Toby tilted his head to the side, then said, "I wish you were staying longer."

He gave a dazzling smile. "You could even spend the time in my suite. I would love having you with me. There is plenty of space and I won't touch you unless you want me to." He grinned at her. "Just kidding."

"Yeah, right."

A low chuckle shook Toby's chest.

"I'm gonna miss you, Toby," Jordan said softly, seriously and sincerely.

Then just as serious and sincere, Toby replied, "I miss you already."

The announcer's voice on the public address system broke in, announcing the flight departure.

"Well, I guess that's me," she said.

"I guess so."

"Take care of yourself."

"Promise me you will do so as well."

"I promise."

Toby moved closer to Jordan and they embraced each other. When they released one another, he said, "Don't go back to Georgia and fall in love on me, okay."

Jordan smiled, reached into her purse and pulled out a business card. "Give me a call from time to time."

Toby took the card. He really didn't want her to go, yet, he couldn't ask her again to stay. Or, could he? "Jordan, I don't want you to go."

"I know. I don't want to go either, but we'll be in touch."

He pulled her into his arms again. She stared up into his eyes, the eyes of a man who she'd come to care more about than she dared to admit and in her heart she knew she'd like nothing more than to stay there with him for the week—stay there forever, but as the final announcement for her flight came over the system, she said, "I've got to go."

"We'll see each other again."

"I hope so."

She lay against his chest, feeling breathless, her heart beating insanely and her blood thudding in her ears. She heard him swear and hold her tighter moments before his mouth came crashing down on hers in a kiss that was nothing short of spellbinding. As he kissed her, she kissed him back. The kiss was passionate, provocative and before her mind spun out of control with desire, the kiss told her that this wasn't the end for them.

"I love you," he said, against her lips.

"Thank you again for being there for me at one of the most difficult times in my life."

As Toby stared at her, she said, "It's all right for you to cry for your mother, cry for the pain you're feeling for her, for your loss. Give yourself permission to open up, give in to the feelings.

He gave her a surprise look but one of appreciation as well. They'd made such a connection in that one day.

They released each other, Jordan turned to walk away but Toby caught her arm and pulled her back to him again. This time when he kissed her, the kiss was passionate, completely thorough and she responded with a deep hunger of her own.

The kiss ended and Jordan turned and walked away from him across the tarmac to the plane. Toby felt the loneliness surround his heart as he watched her through the plate glass windows, her stilettos clicking on the concrete and up the steps into the plane. At the top of the steps, she turned and although she couldn't see him, she waved because she felt sure he was there, looking at her, watching as she left him. The impulse to run back to him, to feel his strong arms around her again, was so strong that, involuntarily she took one step back down the steps.

"You must come in now and take a seat, ma'am," a stewardess's words pulled Jordan from her daydreams.

Jordan settled in her seat and gazed out the window. Before long, the pilot announced their destination. They'd be arriving in Atlanta in four hours and ten minutes with a continuing flight to Augusta. Within minutes, the flight raced down the runway, lifted off and before long, they were so high in the sky that the island of Montego Bay appeared to be a speck in the huge turquoise waters below.

Jordan barely touched the meal served on the flight, but she did enjoy the movie, Nights in Rodanthe.

CHAPTER 7

    Jordan reached into her carry-on bag on the floor beside her feet, placed it in her lap, removed her sketch pad and pencils and she began flipping through the pages. When she came to the sketch of the dress Toby surprised her with, she ran her fingers over the sketch, a small smile covered her face. She wouldn't have to make it now but would she ever wear it again? It was a beautiful dress, she'd worn it for Toby and oddly enough, she only wanted to wear that dress with Toby! For Toby! Only Toby!

Toby. She couldn't get him out of her mind, but why was she thinking *about him?* She thought. They'd spent one amazingly incredible day together and she couldn't ever remember spending time as special as that with anyone before. Ever! That last kiss they shared at the airport, their goodbye kiss, was everything a kiss could be and more, much more, but she knew it was just that, a goodbye

The time Jordan and Toby spent together ended too quickly. It was over as it began. No matter what secret feelings she harbored for Toby, she'd have to live with the reality that she'd probably never ever see Toby again and that made her sad. It was then that all the sadness, the hurt, the loss returned in full force, surrounding her. Jordan rested her head back against the seat, closed her eyes and tears trickled down her cheeks. She whispered, "Will this pain go away? Will it ever go away?"

She reached into her purse for a tissue, she saw there weren't any and she used her fingers to brush away the tears. As she turned to get a tissue from her purse, she felt a light touch on her hand. Jordan looked over to see a woman who appeared to be mid to late fifties, short blond hair, striking blue eyes and a warm, inviting smile, holding a box of tissues.

"Thank you," Jordan said, pulling several tissues from the box and wiped away her tears.

"I can't decide whether you're running away from something difficult or returning to it," the woman said, removing her glasses from her eyes.

Jordan looked at her a moment before saying, "I suppose you could say a bit of both." She was just as sad leaving Toby as she was returning to Georgia—and her issues with Frank.

"Ahhh," the woman said.

"I don't mean to sound so mysterious but I've found myself immersed in a dilemma and there's absolutely nothing I can do about it," Jordan said, looking straight ahead.

"Are you sure?"

Jordan was struck by the question. She returned her attention to the woman. "What do you mean?"

"What you don't seem to know about yourself is that a woman like you can have anything she wants. She just has to make up her mind and go after it."

"Could it really be that simple?"

"Absolutely. Honey, if I had your looks when I was your age, I would've set this world on fire."

When Jordan exhaled loudly and looked at the woman, she thought she saw the cutest most mischievous expression on her face and she couldn't stop herself from laughing.

When the laughing stopped, she placed her hand to her mouth and said, "I'm sorry."

"No problem, dear, but it's true," the woman said. "All you have to do is know your worth, know your value."

Jordan stared at the woman a moment, then said, "I'm sorry. I'm Jordan Banks." She extended her hand.

"I'm Meghan Crawford." She accepted Jordan's hand and when they released hands, she asked, "Are you coming or going, dear?"

"I'm on my way home, Augusta," Jordan replied. "I was on vacation but now, it's back to the real world."

"I was in Jamaica visiting a friend," she said and there was that mischievous smile again, "and I miss him already."

"Does your friend live in Jamaica?"

"Yes, born and bred," Meghan said, reached into her purse and pull out a wallet that she opened to a photo of an extremely handsome, apparently younger, African American man. She handed her wallet to Jordan and as she looked at the photo, Meghan said, "Yes, I'm a bit of a cougar. It's not that I was looking for someone younger. It just happened, and I went with it." She paused a moment before saying, "Matt and I met two years ago. We were on the beach in Montego Bay. Our eyes met, he came over, we struck up a conversation and we began to vibe. We spent the entire day getting to know each other, we spent that night together and the next four nights afterwards." She blushed.

"You go girl." Jordan gave Meghan a high five.

"And, we've talked every day since. This girl gets it in. No moral compass here." She gave Jordan another look, then the two women burst out laughing. "It's true," Meghan chuckled, "We simply did what we wanted and what we felt was best for the two of us. We didn't give one damn about what was going on with the rest of the world."

As Jordan looked at Meghan, she thought how liberating it must be to feel so free and uninhabited. It was then that she regretted not having that complete day in paradise with Toby no matter where it led.

She returned her attention to the picture. "He's very handsome," she said, before returning the wallet to

Meghan. "Will you two be visiting each other again soon?"

"Oh, yes. He'll be coming to California next month," she replied, beaming, returning her wallet to her purse.

After Jordan and Meghan talked another fifteen minutes, Meghan picked up the book from her lap and began reading. Jordan sat back in her seat and stared out the window, watching clouds float by, each had Toby's face. After a while, Jordan turned away from the window, picked up her sketch pad and a pencil, she flipped through the pad until she came to a clean page and she began to sketch. Upon completing a number of sketches, she sat back and began to examine them.

"You are a fashion designer?" Meghan inquired.

"No, actually I'm a teacher."

"These sketches are fantastic. Do you have anything on the market?"

"No."

"If I saw those items in stores," Meghan pointed her finger at the images, "I'd definitely support your line. They're really quite wonderful."

"You would buy some of my designs?"

"Absolutely I would. I like everything that I see here."

"I want you to remember that if and when you see the label, Jordan Dakota Banks on the racks," Jordan teased, giggling.

"No doubt about it. Then I can say I knew you when."

The two women chuckled.

"You really should be with some design house. If this is your passion," she pointed her hand toward the sketch pad, "why are you putting it off, honey? You should be doing the things you want to do with your life. It would be wise to make the best of it while you can. As they say, life is short." Megan Crawford had a beautiful twinkle in her gorgeous, wise eyes. "Honey, sometimes, we just gotta take the plunge, step outside the box." She winked at Jordan. "That's when things happen."

"Sometimes it's not worth the risk."

"You won't know if you don't try. You are a young. beautiful, intelligent woman. Don't waste time doing things that your heart isn't completely in? Do what makes you happy, Jordan. Do it now so that you don't look back tomorrow with regrets. Take it from me, follow your heart, live your dream."

Jordan looked over at her seatmate. "Someone else told me that just the other day."

"Then, I'd say someone is trying to tell you something." Megan Crawford smiled.

A while later, Jordan looked down at the sketch pad in her lap and thought, *One day, someone will be wearing my designs.* After a moment, she lifted her eyes and looked out the window at the blue skies with patches of white clouds floating by and she wondered whether Toby was thinking about her.

www.ingramcontent.com/pod-product-compliance
Lightning Source LLC
Chambersburg PA
CBHW031940240626
47153CB00003B/803